I0594046

TAKING A RISK

JEN TALTY

JUPITER PRESS

Copyright © 2019 by Jen Talty

All rights reserved.

No part of this book may be reproduced in any form or by any electronic or mechanical means, including information storage and retrieval systems, without written permission from the author, except for the use of brief quotations in a book review.

1

The bar smelled of whiskey poured over a heavy serving of sex. Women with their cleavage hanging out leaned over the counter, pushing their boobs up to their chins, trying to get the attention of any football player. The preseason for the Miami Wildcats in any local watering hole was like taking dogs in heat to a dog park on a hot summer day.

Jessica Roads twisted her long blonde hair into a ponytail. She'd moved to Florida two years ago after accepting a position in the marketing department as the online social media coordinator for the Miami Wildcats organization. The move from Virginia had been a difficult one, leaving all her family and friends behind. But then she'd met the man she believed was her soulmate.

She no longer believed in fate.

Glancing over her shoulder, she saw Robert and his wife in the back corner gazing at each other like they were the only ones in the room. Of all the places her ex could go hang out, he chose the one place he knew she might actually frequent.

Was she his ex? He'd been married when they met, though she had no idea for almost a year. She shook her head. Under no circumstances was she dumb.

Just blind.

"Can you believe these women?" Lilliana Foster asked as she plopped herself down on the barstool. "I was in the bathroom, and one went on and on about how hot our boss is, and I'm like girls, he's madly in love with his wife."

"Yeah, but come on, Alex Watson is one hell of a sexy man," Jessica said, twirling her hair, trying not to look over her shoulder. It had been a few months since she'd seen Robert, and the last time it hadn't been pretty.

At least twenty men from the team were in the bar. Some picking up women, others with their girl-friends, others just hanging out, letting off steam. It was only two weeks until the first preseason game, and the boys were restless. She glanced around, noting who was there. Her job didn't require her to check out what happened outside the stadium, but this gave her some insight into the players, helping her to make them more human in a hundred and forty characters.

"Married men are so not sexy to me. And no way should they be to you." Lilliana worked in the advertising department and had become one of Jessica's only two friends in Miami. Jessica had promised herself she'd get out and meet more people, instead of crying over a lying, cheating asshole.

"Now, Nolan Greer is one hell of a sexy man." Lilliana kissed her thumb and forefinger and made a smacking noise.

"He might be sexy, but he barely speaks to anyone, except for yelling out plays in practice. I wonder if he's going to be as hotheaded with refs as a coach as he was as a player." Jessica had interviewed everyone on the team, including coaches, but the new offensive coordinator had yet to give her the time of day.

"I think his aloofness makes him even hotter."

Jessica laughed. "I wouldn't call him aloof. I'd say he's more like the brooding, angry type. He almost never smiles, and every interview I've seen with the man, he has no personality. He answers the questions about the game or his performance, but if you ask him about anything personal or family? He responds with an 'I don't discuss that' or 'let's keep it to the field.'" However, she could get lost in his emerald eyes. They were like pools of aqua spring water, hot and steamy.

Lilliana scowled. "Robert's here, and with the ball and chain too."

"I noticed them the second we stepped foot in this place, and I would prefer to pretend he didn't exist."

"Why didn't you say something? We could have left." Lilliana looped her arm around Jessica, kissing her cheek.

"Because I'm not going to let him stop me from having a good time." While she enjoyed Lilliana's company, she couldn't honestly say the evening had been any fun, but only because of Robert. Every time she saw him, the sting of being made a fool of cut through her pride, and now she second-guessed every man she met, making it impossible to date without thinking they were either married or hiding some twisted, dark secret.

"Then move, because here they come."

Shit.

"Hi, Jessica," Robert said. "Maggs, you remember Jessica, don't you?"

"The charity event with the football team, yes?" Maggs batted her long brown lashes.

The nerve of that man to say hello to his ex-mistress in front of his wife. Poor woman. Jessica had to wonder if she knew about her husband's cheating ways. Or did she turn a blind eye?

"Robert," Maggs said. "I need to use the ladies' room."

"I'll bring the drinks back to the table, darling."

Jessica stared at the woman's swollen belly. Fury bubbled from the pit of her stomach to her throat, and it was about to erupt in word vomit. She waited until his wife was out of sight. "You're a fucking piece of work. Your wife is pregnant, and you waltz her over here in front of your ex-mistress? I have a mind to tell her what a cheating bastard you are." Jessica waved the bartender over. "I need another and get me a couple shots of Fireball."

"Take it easy on that stuff," Robert said. "You don't handle hard liquor well."

"Fuck off. My boyfriend won't like seeing you standing anywhere near me. He knows all about you, and I doubt he'll be as considerate as I am of your wife's feelings."

Robert's eyes went wide before turning into narrowed slits. He turned on his heel and left.

"That man is an asshole."

"I feel so sorry for his kid," Lilliana said.

Jessica tossed her head back, dumping the shot into her mouth, letting it linger as it slowly slid down her throat in a brutal burn. She certainly was over him, but she wasn't over the humiliation she had felt that night he'd seen him and his wife at an event that he had to know she'd attend. "Except I just told him I had a boyfriend and that he'd be here any minute."

Lilliana grinned, and her eyebrows waggled like they always did when she had a crazy idea. "I dare you to kiss the next guy who walks through that door."

"Don't dare me." Jessica had always enjoyed a good dare, and most of the time, she'd do them if they weren't too outlandish. With one more shot, that dare was something she could do, especially if it meant showing Robert she was soooooo over him.

She threw back the other shot, then took out her ponytail and fluffed her hair, praying the next guy was God's gift to women. Standing only five feet from the door, she watched it as someone slowly pulled it back. Staring at a pair of sexy feet wearing flip-flops, she let her eyes take in thick muscular calves, then a pair of pink golf shorts. She didn't have to look any further than this man's formfitting shirt, showing off his taut stomach, to close the gap between them.

Flinging her arms around his thick, broad shoulders, she thought she heard Lilliana call her name, telling her to stop, or maybe don't stop.

Jessica blinked quickly, catching a glimpse of familiar sea-green eyes, before landing her mouth on his soft plump lips.

His rock-hard body went rigid as she tried to coax him into kissing her back.

But he didn't move.

She darted her tongue across his lips and felt a moan vibrate from his throat to her mouth. His strong arms wrapped around her waist as he thrust his tongue inside, taking over the kiss like a wild animal trying to get out of his cage.

Or in this case, get in it.

He demanded more as his hands pressed firmly on her back, pulling her closer.

Her chest heaved into his as she struggled to breathe. The room spun around her in a haze of green and gold. The chatter of people talking phased into a low hum like an engine waiting to be revved. He slowed the kiss, stroking the inside of her mouth like a soft brush hovering over the canvas, waiting for the artist to make that first mark. Her mind formed a picture of the man she'd seen for barely a second before. Soft-green eyes. Short brown hair, almost buzzed on the side with the top longer, and a thick wave...*fuck, I'm kissing Nolan Greer.*

Double fuck. He's kissing me back.

She pried her lips from his, keeping her eyes closed tight. Not only did she not want to look at him, she figured all of his players were staring. Her cheeks flushed.

"One way to get that interview," he whispered into her ear.

"I'm sorry." The words came out in a throaty pant. "Will you please just pretend to be my boyfriend for like the next half hour?" God, this had to be the second dumbest thing she'd ever done. The first one had been believing Robert's lies about why he couldn't spend the night most of the time or be with her on Valentine's Day. What a fool she'd been.

"Why would I do that?"

She shouldn't have had that second shot.

She shouldn't have taken the dare.

"So, I can show my ex I've moved on, that I am over him and couldn't care less about him." She really needed to shut up. Robert was right about one thing: hard liquor wasn't her friend.

"I think I can handle that."

She cocked her head back, opening her eyes, her hands still on his shoulders.

"Just like that? The elusive, antisocial, hotheaded Coach Greer is going to play along?" Did that babble actually fly from her mouth? Yeah, he was going to want to pretend to be like a bee and buzz off.

"I'm not antisocial." His lips drew into a smile, creating a single dimple in his right cheek. His hands still roamed her back in a seductive motion. "But I'll concede to being the other two."

She pursed her lips, staring into those damn eyes.

He chuckled. "The starting quarterback is staring at us from across the room, along with three other young men I coach. The chick in advertising has her mouth gaping wide open. So, I either play along, or you and I have some serious explaining to do."

"We're going to have to do that anyway."

"Maybe we won't." He winked. "Come on. Let me buy my girlfriend a drink."

People really needed to learn not to dare her.

$\mathcal{N}$olan had been a rising running back until he busted his kneecap for the second time. The injury wasn't necessarily career-ending, but Nolan knew he'd never be the same.

However, that wasn't the only reason he'd decided it was time to move on to something else, and thanks to the Miami Wildcats' groundbreaking education program, he'd already had a plan in place for when he did retire.

Only he hadn't thought it would be at the ripe old age of thirty.

He stood behind the beautiful social-media-queen-of-Dolphins, as the guys on the team called her, with his arm draped over her shoulders. Jessica had been the first person he saw the moment he stepped onto the Dolphins' field, and he remembered every detail of that encounter. She had been sitting on the players' bench, computer on her lap, phone in one hand. She had just finished interviewing a couple of the new players, but he hadn't known that at the time.

She'd worn a pair of white slacks and a dark tank top, much like the one she had on tonight. Actually, she always wore the damn things, which caused a slight tightness in his groin.

He had leaned against the railing separating the stands from the players and continued to admire the blonde-haired beauty. At first, he thought she might be one of the cheerleaders, so when she approached him with her sexy smile and sweet-almond eyes, he'd acted like an asshole, not letting her explain who she was or what she did for the team.

He'd always been a standoffish man, keeping his work and private life separate for many reasons. But the day his ex-girlfriend called, telling him she was in kidney failure and would most likely not live and that she needed him to take care of his one-year-old daughter, Nolan's life changed in another unexpected way. Heather had been the real reason he'd retired and became the offensive coordinator for the Miami Wildcats.

He leaned in, trying not to inhale too sharply the coconut scent coming from Jessica's hair that he wanted to tangle his fingers in. "So, where's this jerk?" If it had been any other woman who'd kissed him like that, he would have pushed her aside, then said something direct and to the point but not too rude. He'd spent half his career trying to stay out of the limelight when it came to the press. At first, it had been because he truly hated being the center of attention. But as he got older, he hated what the press could do to a person.

"Sitting to your right in the far corner table with a petite brunette with her tongue thrust down his throat," Jessica said.

The sharp tone of resentment pained him. Not so much because she was angry, but that it seemed she was still hung up on the man.

"You mean like we were doing a few minutes ago?"

She snapped her head in his direction, narrowing her eyes. "I might have started it, but you did the shoving, remember?"

He laughed, waving at the bartender and ordering a round of drinks. "After someone licked my lips." He kissed her cheek, telling himself he did it for the benefit of her ex, but in reality, he wanted to see what her response would be.

She rewarded him with a smile.

"Thanks for the drink," Lilliana said.

"My pleasure." He glanced over his shoulder, catching sight of the couple she'd described. Her ex turned his head the moment he'd made eye contact.

Coward.

"Those are some big-ass tits."

Jessica nudged him in the ribs with her elbow. "You're not supposed to be staring at her; besides, she's pregnant, so she had a little help from mother nature."

He glided his fingers under her hair, tickling the back of her neck. He understood her bitter tone. "You're much prettier than she is."

"Thanks, I appreciate the compliment." Jessica looked up at him with those sexy, golden-brown eyes and long lashes.

He continued to keep one hand on her neck and shoulders, constantly gliding them over her smooth, silky skin. She'd been making him uncomfortable for weeks now, but standing next to her, touching her, he felt totally at ease.

Only his dick wanted to stand at attention.

"Oh shit, no," Jessica said, holding her phone up.

"Brad wants to know if he should snap a picture of us so I can post it on the team account."

"You wouldn't dare? Would you?" Nolan asked. In all his career, he'd done his very best to keep the women he dated out of the spotlight, even the fake ones.

Now that he had Heather, it was even more important. He couldn't let the media make a circus out of his life...nor his daughter's.

"Never say those words to her," Lilliana said, holding up her drink. "Unless you want her to, because a dare is how she landed in a lip-lock with you."

Jessica pursed her lips, shaking her head. "I'm not going to post a picture, and he's a good friend, so I'll shoot him a text back about what's going on." She looked up at Nolan and smiled. "Don't worry. Every-thing that happens here tonight, stays here."

"Thanks." He swallowed, reminding himself he'd come here to see her, hang with the team, and stop being so distant with everyone, as his new boss recommended.

"But I hadn't thought this through. Hell, it didn't even register with me that I was kissing you."

Ouch.

He arched a brow. "Exactly who did you think

you were jumping then?" This should be good, he thought.

"A guy with sexy feet, in pink shorts, with green eyes. But I recognized them, so I knew it was you, but not until after the kiss started."

"Sexy feet, huh?" He set his beer on the bar, turning the stool to face him, reminding himself that he could have a night out and that didn't make him a bad son or a bad father. Kissing a woman wouldn't be the end of his world, as long as it was kept private.

He ignored the tickle in his brain that told him he was standing in a public place.

"Now this time, know it's me before we kiss." Resting his hands on her bare thighs, just below her shorts, he pushed his broad body between her legs. He smiled as she locked gazes with him. Her eyelids fluttered when he cupped the back of her neck, threading his fingers in her hair, tilting her head slightly, parting her luscious lips.

She let out a soft moan when his mouth connected with hers like two ends of a magnet. Her tongue greeted his with a swirl, sending electricity from his head to his toes. Her firm thighs flexed as he teased the skin just under the hem of her black shorts.

It had been two years since his mouth had been

anywhere near a woman, and his body reacted to her touch with a powerful hunger he'd thought he'd lost.

"Get a room, Coach," a male voice shouted from somewhere in the back.

He jerked his head back, but the rest of his body remained pressed against hers.

"That was the third-string quarterback, wasn't it?" he whispered, forcing his breath to remain even. His mind told him to back away from the woman. His body said something entirely different.

Currently, his body won the tug of war.

"Actually, it was the rookie field goal kicker, not that it makes a difference." She kept her gaze locked with his, which didn't help the pounding of his heart, nor the thought of scooping her up and carrying her out the door to his car where he doubted he'd be able to control himself.

"Robert and his wife are heading this way," Lilliana said.

"Wife?" Nolan sucked in a breath, remembering his only role was to make another man jealous. The moment he walked out of this bar, his fake relationship would be over, which shouldn't matter.

But it did.

Worse, he'd come here tonight because he'd

overheard her saying she'd be here, and he wanted a chance to talk to her in a different setting.

Nolan eyed Jessica's ex, making sure he conveyed a strong message to the weasel. The woman he'd married was probably nice enough, but still, don't cheat, assuming he'd married the woman he'd cheated on Jessica with.

Robert stole a glance over his shoulder as he ushered his wife out the front door. For good measure, Nolan kissed Jessica's temple while keeping eye contact with the asshole.

"Hey, good-looking. Can I buy you a drink?" a man asked as he leaned in next to Lilliana.

"Sure," she said.

Nolan wanted to thank the man for distracting Lilliana so he could focus on Jessica, who had turned her head with questioning eyes.

"You okay?" He knew he should swivel the barstool, removing himself from between her legs, but he couldn't any more than he could stop caressing her thigh.

"I'm just glad they left. Thanks for being a sport about this. I put you in an awkward position with the team, just because I don't want some asshole who doesn't deserve me to think I've been sitting around pining over him."

"Have you?" He carefully studied her facial expressions, hoping he'd be able to read how she really felt about her ex, but she just blinked.

"I'm still angry at what he did to me."

He arched a brow. "What exactly was that?"

"That, my friend, is a loaded question."

Normally, he wasn't the kind to pry. He valued his privacy and respected others'. "I'm all ears."

She shook her head, letting out a long sigh, and looked everywhere but at him. "I didn't know he was married."

"What the fuck?" He stepped back, staring at her. "Does his wife know about you?"

She eased back on the stool, swiveling toward the bar, shame written all over her face. "I have no idea what she knows or doesn't know."

HIS PHONE BUZZED. He pulled it from his back pocket and read a text from his dad.

CALL me as soon as you can.

. . .

"I'M SORRY. I've got to take this." He gave Jessica a quick kiss on the lips before racing outside, pressing the contact information for his father.

It rang once.

"Nolan," his father's voice boomed from the cell phone speaker.

"What's wrong, Dad? Is Heather okay?"

"I think she's handling this better than I am." His father made a sniffling sound. "It's Mom; she's not doing well and is asking for you."

When Nolan had retired two seasons ago, he knew he wanted to coach, so he spent a year learning from some of the best. When it came time to send out résumés, he'd been looking more up north, until his father had called with the bad news.

Stage four ovarian cancer.

"I'll be there in less than thirty minutes."

3

*J*essica stood next to Brad Michaels, the team photographer, as he snapped pictures of specific players that would be featured in this week's blog and on the website. She had all the interviews done.

But one.

She stuffed her hand in her back pocket, pulling out the handwritten note she'd found taped to her office door.

JESSICA,

. . .

Sorry I left without saying goodbye. Family emergency. How about, after practice, I give you that interview you've been bugging me about?

See you on the field,
  Nolan

"Take a bunch of Coach Greer. I'm going to do a special feature on the newest member of the coaching staff." She eyed Nolan as he ran some plays with his offense. He wore athletic shorts that came down to his knees and a muscle tank top with the Dolphins' logo on the front. His thick biceps flexed as he tossed the ball back to the second-string quarterback.

Ditching her at the bar two nights ago stung more than she cared to admit, especially since he'd left right after she'd told him she'd been a mistress.

The talk around the water cooler this morning had been about her and Nolan. Not a single person said anything to her about it, which she'd been grateful for since her pride couldn't take another hit at having to admit she'd just used the sexy coach to make her ex jealous.

Only now she couldn't stop thinking about Nolan. She licked her lips.

"You do know he doesn't like interviews, right? As a player, he avoided them, even when he'd broken a few league records." Brad had been the team photographer for the last five years, and he'd been more than helpful to her the first season. "Oh, wait, you must know that since you were making out with him the other night."

"Thanks for the reminder," she muttered as she raised her pen to her lips, remembering how his hot tongue gently stroked them before roping her tongue into his intoxicating mouth.

That man could kiss a girl till she fainted as if she'd been out in the sun too long.

Nolan bent on one knee. Some of his players did the same thing, while others stood, leaning over other players to see the play route. Over the week-end, she'd re-read all the articles about his career. Watched videos of his more memorable moments, both good and bad, along with the few interviews he'd been forced to give over the years.

Short and to the point, and almost never answering questions about his family or personal life, especially when it came to girlfriends and women. A few pictures surfaced here and there with speculation about the woman in the photos, but either his love life had been nonexistent, or he'd been the only football player she'd ever met that didn't kiss and tell.

"Do you want a portrait of Greer?" Brad asked.

"Just action shots."

Nolan stood, smacking the shoulder pads of one of the new recruits as they walked toward the sidelines.

The sun hung low over the stadium as the dinner hour approached. The players jogged off the field while the coaches stood around, talking to one another.

She waited patiently in the third row of the stands, her laptop out and opened to the list of questions she had for Nolan. She checked the battery on her phone, making sure it wouldn't die while she recorded the session.

"Hey." Nolan jogged up the steps. "You got my note."

"I did." She raised her hand, shielding the sun from her eyes. "I hope all is well with your family."

He sat down, leaving a seat between them. His normally clean-shaven face sported a scruffy new look. Dark circles lined his eyes. He ran his hand down his face, his forefinger and thumb coming together at his squared chin. "I don't want anything about my family to be in the article unless I say it's okay, and I won't answer personal questions."

"We'll just cover your career." She reached out to touch the side of his face but retracted quickly. "What's wrong?" she asked softly.

He turned his head, squinting at the sun. "I'm telling you this because I honestly want you to understand why I left the other night."

"Considering the timing, I figured it had to do with my confession."

"I was taken off guard by that, but no. That was not why I left," he said. "My mother has stage four ovarian cancer, and the other night when I left without saying goodbye, my father called to tell me that my mother was asking for me. We're trying to make her as comfortable as possible, but the end is near." He rubbed his eyes harshly. "I'm trying to hold it together for my dad, who is losing it."

"Oh, Nolan." She placed her hand on his shoulder. "I'm so sorry. That can't be easy on anyone in the family."

"It pretty much sucks." He yanked his baseball cap off and ran his thick fingers through his dark-brown hair. "I'm living at home until she passes. My sister's there too."

"Why aren't you taking some time off? I'm sure everyone would understand." She found herself massaging his firm muscles, trying to ease the tension from his body. She wanted to wrap her arms around him and hold him. She had no idea what it was like to lose a parent, and from the sadness etched in his eyes, she dreaded the day she'd have to go through it.

He turned his head, and they locked gazes. "Because my mother wants me to work, but she knows I'll come home if she needs me."

"You're a good man, Nolan Greer."

"Thank you." The corners of his lips turned upward slightly. He took her hand and kissed it. "I really am sorry about the other night. I never got the chance to get your number and have felt bad about it all weekend."

"I think you've had other things on your mind, so don't think twice about it."

"But I did." He continued to hold her hand, his thumb gently caressing her palm. "When I got in the car to go to my parents, I thought, I need to text Jessica, but then I realized I didn't have your number, and Alex wouldn't give it to me."

"You actually called Alex Watson?" Her breath hitched.

He nodded. "I hope you don't think it's too creeperish."

"No more than me randomly kissing you." She smiled. "We can do this interview another time, if you want." She didn't want to put it off, not because it was so important it had to be done right now, but she was being selfish and wanted to spend a little more time with him, even if it was only asking him about his career and why the change to coaching.

"Nope. Besides, it would look bad if I was the only coach that you didn't feature before the season starts."

She pulled her hand from his and held up her phone. "Do you mind if I tape it?"

"Not at all, but would it be possible for me to get a copy before it goes live?"

"I always send out a proof. If there is anything you don't like, we can change it."

"I appreciate that."

"Okay." She tapped her phone. "Interview with Nolan Greer, offensive coordinator of the Miami Wildcats. Why'd you want to be a football player?"

He let out a hearty laugh. "My dad signed me up for Pop Warner when I was six. Not sure there was a reason why, but a bunch of the neighbor kids were doing it. The first game came around, and they had to weigh me." He shook his head, smiling. "I thought I was something special since I was the only one, but I found out later they were concerned I wasn't big enough. I forget what you had to weigh, but I was a tiny kid at maybe fifty pounds soaking wet. But from that first weigh-in, I was hooked."

"I can't imagine you being a small kid. Do you have a picture? Would you be willing to let me use it?"

"I'll see if I can dig one up."

She glanced at her computer screen, scrolling through the questions. "Why a running back?"

"Like every little boy, I wanted to be the quarterback, but during drills, it turned out I was faster than anyone on the team, so I started at that position. In middle school, they moved me around a bit as I started to grow. But my speed, agility, and the fact it takes a lot to bring me down, brought me back to the position."

The majority of the questions she'd put in her Word document had been related to his career, and very little on the personal side because she had already known he'd want it that way. But she wanted to know more about the man and figured the fans of the Dolphins wanted that as well. She could do that without asking anything about family.

Or girlfriends.

"My brother played soccer when he was little. He had this pair of underwear that he'd hide because he didn't want my mother to wash the luck out of them. Did you have any rituals in football growing up?" She looked at him as he cocked his head.

"I know very few professional athletes that don't have some kind of ritual."

"Will you share with us one of yours?"

He smiled. "It started with my first game my freshman year in high school when the starter was sick, and Coach put me in. I was scared to death. The quarterback, who was a senior, came up to me and told me to just relax. He smacked my helmet, and for whatever reason, I grabbed his mask and facebutted him. He was not happy with me."

"What did he do?"

"What could he do? I was his teammate and currently the kid he had to count on to step it up." Nolan smiled. "So, the next game, I had to start again. He walked up to me, and before he could say anything, I grabbed his mask and did it again, and then said, 'we won last time, so I thought this should be our thing.' I've done that with every quarterback of every game I ever started."

The ease at which he spoke should calm her,

only it sent her stomach on a tumble. "You won the state champions in high school twice, correct?"

His big smile quickly lowered into something humble, and he nodded.

"You were named MVP one year, right?"

"We win as a team; we lose as a team. For every great play I had, someone else had to do something extraordinary to make it happen."

She admired the way he treated his victories versus how he talked about his experiences as a player. She wanted to talk to him about that some more but thought it might be too personal. "There was more than one college that tried to recruit you, and you were high in the draft. How did it feel being one of the top round picks?"

"Honestly, it felt good, but I don't like to be the center of attention, and there were many talented football players in that draft, so I focused on the game, not the media circus."

For a man who didn't like interviews, he did them incredibly well.

"Could you pick one highlight of your career that affected you the deepest?"

"The game I blew out my knee for the second time. It was bittersweet. There were ten seconds left in the game, and if we didn't score a touchdown, we'd lose, and that meant we wouldn't be in the playoffs. Twelve yards from the goal line, fourth down, and the play called for me to charge forward."

"I watched the footage from that game." She cringed, rubbing her own knee.

He chuckled, then turned somber. "The play didn't go off as planned, and I had to scramble. I remember running right, then making that quick turn up field. I felt something snap in my leg, but I pushed through it. When I watch that video clip, and the way I was limping, I can't believe I dodged two tackles." He shook his head, his hand over his kneecap, massaging it. "But it was the one I didn't dodge as I crossed the goal line that sealed my fate."

"The other player dove at you, tackling you low."

"It was a good tackle, and had I not already been injured during the play, it wouldn't have been but another bruise to an already banged-up body. I think the hardest part about that win was I couldn't walk off the field, and the victory for my teammates was hushed because of it."

She stared at him for a long moment. His green eyes flickered like fireflies on a warm summer night. "People have accused you of retiring too early. That perhaps you had another few good years in you."

"I've got many good years left in me." He winked.

"As a coach. I'm lucky that I had a plan for when I retired, because at some point, it will happen to every player, whether it be injury or age."

"It's rumored that you had a few job opportunities, including a few colleges. Why Miami Wildcats?"

"I have a lot of respect for the organization and the way they do business. Also, I grew up here, and my parents and sister still live here, so I get to be closer to my family." He smiled, but there was glimmer of a tear in the corner of his eye.

She figured it was best to change the direction of the interview. "Being on the field as a player and being a coach are very different. How are you handling that?" She scanned her questions, trying to find ones that would give the readers insight, making Nolan more human and less standoffish, which often pointed the media right at a person.

"As a player, I focused on two things, running and scoring. As a coach, I need to focus on the bigger picture and work with my offense to make the right calls at the right time, which hasn't been easy for me." He smiled, adjusting his baseball cap and looking across the field. "There seem to be bets on how long it will take before I shoot my mouth off in the heat of the game, since as I player I tended to get in the ref's face when I didn't like his call."

She laughed, remembering some of the footage of his more colorful moments. "You did take a few unsportsmanlike penalties."

"My temper was my biggest weakness as a player. I'm hoping I don't carry that habit into my coaching." He reached out, resting his hand on the back of her chair.

She swallowed. "What do you think, as a coach, will be your biggest asset to this team?"

"I honestly have no idea. It's my first experience coaching, and I've been given a huge role. Ask me that question at the end of the season, and I might have an answer."

"I think we can end here." She turned the voice recorder off and shut her laptop down. She could have kept the conversation going for hours, asking the same question, but in a different way, just so she could listen to his voice and look into his warm eyes. "I should have this done by Wednesday."

"Great." He glanced at his Apple Watch. "I'm sorry, but I've got to get going to my parents' house."

"Sure, no problem." She stuffed everything in her backpack. "I'm really sorry about your mom. If there is anything I can do to help, just call me."

"I need your number to do that." He winked, handing her his unlocked phone.

Luckily, her hands didn't shake as she put her number in, then texted herself so she'd have his. "I mean it. I know some people say those kinds of things because its polite, but really, anything you need, just let me know."

"I will probably take you up on that offer." He leaned in and kissed her cheek. His lips warm and soft. His breath moist.

Her body shivered. Her goosebumps had goosebumps.

"I'll see you tomorrow," he whispered.

A warm tingle shot up her spine. Two weeks ago, Nolan barely gave her the time of day, but now he was kissing her on the cheek and being playful. There wasn't a single person on the field, so it wasn't for show. She blinked. The only reason for kissing him had been to rub it in Robert's face.

Robert wasn't here either.

Nolan sauntered toward the building where the coaches' offices were. His hips swayed in a subtle yet distinct movement that showed his confidence.

She needed to find a good excuse to call him after the article was published.

4

*N*olan stared at the screen on his laptop. The article Jessica had written hadn't been much different than any other, and he appreciated her sticking to his guidelines. She did have a flare for words, and her humor mixed with a serious tone lent itself well for an entertaining yet informative read. There wasn't one word he'd change.

He brought up his email.

Jessica,

The article is great as it is. I see no need to change anything.

. . .

"Screw that," he mumbled, checking the time. It wasn't six yet, so maybe she was still in her office. He snagged his phone and quickly pulled up her contact information. For the last few days, he hadn't seen much of her, mostly because he left right after practice. She'd come down to the field a couple of times, and they waved to each other and smiled, but that was about it.

"Hello?" she answered in a huff.

"Hey, its Nolan."

He heard a rattling of some kind, almost like metal against metal. "Shit," she muttered. "Sorry."

"What's wrong?"

"Flat freaking tire."

"Where are you?" He shut his laptop and started packing up his things.

"Parking lot."

"I'll be right there."

He didn't wait for an answer as he flung his back-pack over his shoulder and ignored the dull ache in his knee as he jogged down the hallway. As soon as he pushed open the double doors, he spotted the sexy social-media-queen-of-Dolphins bent over, trying to unscrew a lug nut, her long hair flowing down toward the ground.

He paused for a moment, staring at her adorable

rear end, wanting to come up behind her and give one of those cheeks a nice little smack. He cleared his throat, and then cleared his mind of sexual visuals that drove him mad.

"Let me do that," he said.

She jumped, causing her to lean forward and hit her head on the side of her SUV.

"Oh...crap," she moaned, grabbing her forehead.

"Sorry." He lunged forward, grabbing her hips, twisting her to face him. Holding her again sent signals to all the nerve endings in his body. He glided his hands to the small of her back, drawing her closer to him. The sweet smell of coconut filled his nostrils.

Her lashes fluttered, showing off her soft, brown eyes glowing in the sunlight.

"You okay?"

"Yeah, I think I'll live." She scrunched her face and continued to rub the top of her head.

He curled his fingers around her delicate wrist, placing her hand on his shoulder. His heart pounded in his chest as if he'd sprinted across the entire football field.

Her dazed and confused looked amused him... and aroused him. He kissed her forehead, then her temple, gliding his lips to the sensitive spot behind her earlobe.

"What are you doing?" she whispered.

"Making sure you're not hurt." He lifted his head, staring into her sweet eyes once again. The moment she entered his personal space, he wanted to devour her, tucking her away from the rest of the world, keeping her all to himself. "I didn't mean to startle you." His thumbs drew little circles on the small of her back, just under her damned tank top. A red one this time, but also more stylish, going with her black slacks.

Her breath came in choppy pants as her breasts pushed against his chest, her eyes wide. Beautiful would be the understatement of the year. Stunning didn't quite do it either.

"I'm fine."

If he didn't pull it back now, there was no telling what he'd do, and the last thing he needed right now was to deal with a new relationship. He'd never be able to spend any time with her since he was either working or spending time with his family.

Family first.

That was the Greer motto and one he was damn proud of, especially right now when his parents needed him the most.

Heather would always need him, and she'd always come first, which meant women weren't an option right now.

"You're incredible," he whispered, leaning in as she licked her pink lips. He caught her tongue, sucking it into his mouth. She tasted like sunshine and warm honey. He told himself he'd count to ten and then end the kiss, only he couldn't concentrate enough to get past five.

Her hands pressed against his chest, firmly pushing.

He took a step back, tripping over his backpack he didn't remember dropping. Once he regained his balance, and composure, he lifted his gaze to meet hers.

She covered her mouth.

"I'm sorry," he said for lack of anything else to say. "I shouldn't have done that."

"Why did you?"

He shook his head. "I don't know. Caught up in the moment, remembering the last time we kissed. Could have been because I'm sleep deprived and not handling things with my folks too well."

Her wide eyes narrowed as her body recoiled like a snake.

"That didn't come out right."

"No, it didn't," she said, folding her arms. "Then again, I kissed you the first time to get back at Robert, so let's call it even."

He laughed. "I can live with that." He snagged the wrench. "Where's the spare?"

"Right here." She pulled a tire from the trunk.

It lacked firmness and after closer consideration, she had a second problem. "That's not going to work." He took the tire from her hands and examined it. Not many cars had actual tires these days for spares. "Look." He pointed to a nail in the spare tire. "You're going to need to have it towed to a tire shop."

"Wonderful," she muttered. "That is going to cost a small fortune."

"You don't have roadside assistance?"

She shook her head.

"I can call the garage that works on my family's cars. Maybe they can cut you a deal." Since it was his cousin's shop, it would be the deal of the century.

"I'd really appreciate that." She took out her phone. "Thank God for Uber."

"Where do you live?" He tossed the tire back into her car, then lowered the jack. No matter where she called home, he'd be taking her there. "I can give you a ride if it's near my folks."

"A couple blocks from Concert Hall, but I don't want to put you out."

"Put your phone away. I go right past you." It wasn't a lie, thankfully.

"What about my car?"

"I'll make sure it's taken care of. Don't leave anything of value in it and put the keys over the visor." He shot his cousin a quick text, explaining the situation.

"But how do you know it will be safe?"

He stared at his phone for a few minutes. His cousin was generally quick to respond to an SOS from family. Nolan smiled at the single emoji thumbs-up.

"Because the tow truck is on the way." He flung his backpack over his shoulder and winked. "Trust me."

He told himself he was doing what any other good person would do, and giving her a ride had nothing to do with wanting to spend more time with her and finding excuses to touch her, as he helped her into his full-sized SUV.

"Nice ride," she said, crossing her legs. God, how he wanted to press his lips on those sexy ankles. "Why not a pickup?"

He found himself wanting to explain that he'd

traded in his pickup when he decided he couldn't give Heather up for adoption. He'd fallen in love with his little girl the moment he found out of her existence. To him, she was perfect in every way. "I need a—"

His phone ringer blaring over the car speakers stopped him mid-sentence.

"That's my dad. I have to take it." But he wasn't doing it over the Bluetooth. He took his phone, putting in his earbud. "What's up, Dad?" He glanced at Jessica, who looked out the window, twirling her hair, ignoring him. He had half a mind to pull over and step out of the SUV so he could have this conversation in private.

"Heather tripped playing in the yard with Muffy."

Nolan sucked in a deep breath. His daughter had his drive… and his lack of fear.

"Is she hurt?" But he knew the answer as soon as he heard his little girl's cry in the background.

"Her wrist looks pretty swollen. I'm taking her to the Urgent Care by my office."

"I can be there in ten." He glanced at Jessica, who looked out at the window as if she weren't hearing his half of the conversation.

"You'll beat us," his father said. "She wants to talk to you."

"Daddy!" Heather said between thick sobs. "Don't be mad. I didn't mean to fall."

"I know you didn't, baby. Daddy's not mad at all. Just worried." Nolan made a right turn, catching Jessica's shocked stare as she snapped her head.

"I'm not a baby," Heather said in her stern voice, then hiccupped again. "Papa won't let me take the ice off, and it's soooooooo cold."

"Papa's a doctor, so you do as he says, okay, munchkin?"

"Yes, Daddy."

"I'll see you in a couple of minutes."

"Okay, Daddy."

"I love you." He took his earpiece out, dropping it into the cupholder, glancing once more at Jessica.

She tilted her chin but said nothing.

"I'm sorry, but I've got to take a detour. My daughter needs an x-ray."

"You have daughter?" Jessica asked, shaking her head. "And no one knows?"

His chest tightened. Very few people outside his closest circle of family and friends knew he had a daughter. His ex-girlfriend, Gina, had been more of a two-week one-night stand. They complemented each other in bed but could barely stand each other after the first week. They had almost nothing in common, except for a healthy appetite for sex.

The affair ended, and he never heard from Gina until she was near death.

"I don't know how long this will take." He pulled into the parking lot of the care center. "You can take my truck, and I can just go home with my dad." He didn't want to make a federal case out of his personal life. He didn't owe her any explanations.

Jessica blinked her eyes a few times.

"Or you can stay to meet her." He swallowed. He hadn't dated since he became a single father, and technically, he still hadn't dated, but was he willing to introduce Jessica to Heather?

Not a good idea, but no sooner did he change his mind than his father pulled into the parking spot across from him.

He stepped from the truck and walked quickly to his father's sedan, opening the rear passenger door.

"Daddy!" Heather's good leg kicked wildly, while the one in the brace moved, but not as fast nor as wild. He knew she needed another operation, and that broke his heart into a million pieces.

"Hey, baby." He unsnapped her car seat, careful

of her wrapped arm. Before picking her up, he wiped away her tears.

"I'm NOT a baby!"

"You'll always be Daddy's little girl." He hoisted her into his arms. "Now give Daddy a kiss."

Heather palmed his cheeks before puckering up her lips. Nothing better than a big, sweet kiss from the most important person in the world.

"Son." His father slapped his shoulder. "I need to get home to Mom."

"We're good. I'll be home as soon as I can." Nolan knew he should have asked his father to drive Jessica home, but he wanted to explain.

When he shifted Heather in his arms, she groaned.

"Still hurt a lot?"

Heather nodded, tucking her face into his neck. "It's a seven."

She'd had two surgeries in the last two years, and she'd learned to give her pain a number.

"Let's get you inside."

"Daddy?" Heather whispered.

"What is it?"

"Who's the lady that's following us?"

He looked over his shoulder and smiled wryly. "That's Jessica. She writes articles for the team."

"She's pretty," Heather whispered.

"Yes, she is."

5

*J*essica normally didn't hide from people, but today she wanted to avoid Nolan as long as possible. She'd taken an Uber from Urgent Care to home right after Heather went to an examination room. Nolan had tried to insist Jessica stay, but that would have been weird on many levels.

She glanced at her phone. Three texts from Nolan about how her car would be in the parking lot by five and that he had the keys. The fourth had been asking why she hadn't let him drive her to work. She'd responded to that one by saying she had an early meeting. She did have a meeting, but it had been scheduled for nine. That was better than calling him a liar and accusing him of being ashamed of his own daughter.

Nolan was just another man with a lot of secrets, something she couldn't tolerate.

A tap at the door startled her. Glancing up, she let out a sigh of relief to see Lilliana standing in the doorway with a bag of baked chips and a couple of sodas, her standard *I need to talk* food.

Jessica set her laptop to the side. "What's up?"

"What is wrong with me?" Lilliana whined as she plopped herself in the seat on the other side of the desk. "Why can't I land a normal guy like Brad?"

"I told you playing coy was a stupid idea. Just ask him out."

"I'm not normally shy or nervous around men, but something about Brad makes me jittery." Lilliana ripped open the bag of chips and started chomping. She lifted her feet, dumping them on the desk after kicking off her sandals. Lilliana had been a tomboy her entire life. She enjoyed the outdoors and played just about any sport better than most, which often intimidated her dates.

"I find that hard to believe. You can talk to anyone at any time."

"Have you ever seen me pick up a guy?" Lilliana asked.

Jessica had to think about that for a moment. Lilliana had lush, full lips, jet-black hair, and the most stunning ice-blue eyes. Whenever they walked into a bar, heads would turn. Men looked Lilliana up and down, and it was rare she ever had to buy her own drinks.

"No. I guess you're always the one getting hit on."

"Yeah, by players and cheaters, and men with weird fetishes. Nice guys like Brad, I seem to repel like I'm a can of bug spray."

"You're asking the wrong woman for help. I was a mistress and didn't know." And I'm attracted to another liar because if he can lie about his daughter, he can lie about anything. Jessica took a can of diet soda and flicked the metal tab. A loud pop followed a sizzle which filled the room while bubbles from the carbonation floated through the opening. "You've known Brad longer than I have, so I don't think it would be weird if you invited him out for drinks after work or something."

"Except for the fact I almost never see him at work."

Jessica thought about telling Lilliana that Brad would be in her office in less than ten minutes, but then figured Lilliana might bolt. "Make a point of running into him. Come visit me when I'm down on the field."

"I hate it when you make sense." Lilliana dropped her feet to the ground, smoothing down her slacks. "I really don't know why he's got me all wound up into a nervous schoolgirl."

Jessica laughed. "Maybe it's because he's one of the few men who don't fall at your feet."

"I think it has more to do with the fact that I actually like him in a way that could mean something."

"And what something could that be?" Jessica arched a brow. In the two years she'd known Lilliana, she'd gone out with a lot of men. None of them led to any long-lasting relationships. According to her, most of them never even made it to the bedroom.

"Something more than just going out and having a good time. I'm tired of the game."

"Tired of football?" Brad's voice barreled through the room.

Jessica tried to keep a straight face as Lilliana's eyes widened with surprise.

"You love football. It's all you talk about," Brad said, leaning against the doorjamb. "And you come to every game."

"We weren't talking about football." Jessica ignored the narrowed stare from Lilliana. "She's just tired of the dating scene."

The narrowed stare turned into a glower.

"I hear that." Brad stepped across the room, tossing a thumb drive on the desk. "I took some great shots today. I think those will be really good for the blog before the first preseason game."

"Thanks." Jessica twirled the thumb drive in her fingers, smiling at Lilliana, trying to get her to say something. Anything.

"I'm not going to be around until the first game. I've got a couple of freelance contracts I've got to complete, but you know how to reach me."

"I do." Jessica smiled, then turned her attention to Lilliana, who seemed to force a smile. Jessica tried to use her eyes, shifting them toward Brad to coax Lilliana to ask him out, but by her tight lips, it didn't seem like that would happen.

Brad turned toward the door, then glanced over his shoulder. "So, how about we go have drinks or something tonight. We can laugh at the people either trying to pick someone up or out on their first awkward date."

"All of us?" Lilliana asked. Her face tightened even more.

"Well, I suppose, but—"

"I can't go tonight." Jessica didn't think the invitation included her, so she did them both a solid and backed out gracefully.

"Too bad." Brad smiled. "How about you, Lilliana?"

"Tonight?" Lilliana stood, setting the bag of chips on the desk. The lines in her crinkled forehead disappeared, as did the rigidity of her lips.

Brad nodded. "Armory good for you? Say around seven?"

"Perfect." Lilliana swayed toward the door. "I best get back to my office."

Before Lilliana and Brad could get through the door, Nolan stepped in, pushing himself between the couple.

"What the fuck is this?" He lifted up his phone in Brad's face. "Did you take these?"

"No." Brad reached out to take the phone but retracted.

"What is it?" Jessica wanted to tell Nolan to shut up, but she'd learned over the course of the last couple of years that when dealing with football players and the coaching staff, it was better to find out what got their tail in a ruffle.

"It's a picture of you and Nolan in the parking lot yesterday," Brad said, shaking his head. "Another one of you, Nolan, and a little girl, and the last one is Nolan with the same little girl sporting a pink cast on her arm."

"What the hell? Posted somewhere?" She quickly pulled her laptop closer, pulling up all the social media feeds.

"Everywhere, according to my sister who sent me the link." Nolan inched closer to Brad. "If I find out you took these, I'm going to—"

"Back off," Jessica said as she scrolled through some of the feeds, glancing at the comments. "Brad wouldn't do this."

"He's the only one with a camera around here." Nolan inched back a tad but still stood a little too close to Brad, who didn't back down, but the fear of being pummeled was etched in his soft eyes.

"I might have a camera, but I don't post any of the pictures I take for the team. It's in my contract. Team use only."

"Doesn't mean you wouldn't take something like that to sell for a quick buck." Nolan's face turned bright red.

"Shut up, Nolan," Jessica said, focusing on the negative comments and how to fix this preseason scandal. Two comments in the posts she'd read disturbed her the most.

Is the man ashamed of his crippled child? #deadbeatdad

He could have put her in that brace and broken her arm himself. #childbeater

"Nolan, sit." Jessica waved to the chair once occupied by Lilliana. "You other two, leave."

"He's not leaving." Nolan pointed to Brad. "Not until he can prove he didn't take those pictures."

"He has nothing to prove." Jessica tried to keep her voice calm, but inside her vocal cords shook. Her heart raced in one continuous beat. Half of her wanted to scream at Nolan that he'd brought this on himself. She understood wanting to protect his family, but keep a little girl tucked away in a glass bubble? That made him less than a man.

"Maybe you told him to follow us. Take the pictures. Create a scandal to get more likes or press or whatever, and in the process tossed *my* family under the bus."

She sucked in a deep breath, letting it out slowly, counting to three because she'd never make it to ten. She waved Brad and Lilliana out of the room as she stood, closing the door behind them. "That was uncalled for and rude. I won't be treated or talked to like that in my own office. Now, sit."

He inched forward, standing so close she could feel the rage pouring from his veins. "No thanks to you. I can't believe you put my little girl right out there in the middle of my family dealing with my mother dying. This doesn't just hurt the team, it affects my father, his practice, me, and my daughter. I've worked very hard to protect her, then you show up with your stupid little game, and now I'm being called a deadbeat and child abuser. Not to mention I could end up losing my job over all this."

"You're upset. I get it."

"Upset?" He kicked the chair. "I'm fucking furious."

Oh, did she want to lay into him, but she decided to deal with the situation as it related to work, not how she wanted to call him a lying loser.

She adjusted the chair, then stepped behind her desk. "I don't care what you think, but I didn't do anything." She sat, staring at the computer screen. "You can take it out on me all day long, that's fine, but we have three tasks to achieve before you walk out of this office and have to face the media."

He paced between the door and the chair, and it damn near drove her insane.

"What three things?" he asked.

"Come up with a team statement. Come up with a personal story that puts this in perspective." She glanced over her laptop. "One that you can live with, protects your family, but more importantly, shows the real man that you are, not the rash judgments people are making." She absolutely knew he didn't lay a finger on his daughter, but the embarrassment part? Why else would he keep her a secret?

She quickly sent an email to all the appropriate people within the organization, including the spokesperson, that she was aware of the situation and that Coach Greer was in her office. "We'll have company in about twenty minutes, so let's figure this out before they get here."

Nolan sat down, looking at his phone, deep lines forming on his forehead. Anger flared from his narrowed eyes.

But she also saw raw pain.

She shifted in her seat, watching the team social media feeds blow up and emails coming in from the organization. "The team has called a press conference for six. They will give a statement and need you to give one as well."

"Fucking clusterfuck," Nolan muttered, then nodded.

"I think the best way to handle the slanderous statement about you hurting your daughter is to deny it wholeheartedly since it's not true and we can prove that. A short statement, direct and to the point. I'd go as far as to say that continued false attacks on your character could bring lawsuits. I can write it for you."

Again, Nolan nodded. His long fingers rubbed his temples. "I need to protect her from the public eye. She has a surgery scheduled in two months, and I don't need a bunch of reporters hounding my family at the hospital."

Jessica swallowed, her fingers hovering over the keyboard. "I think you should also address Heather's leg and what's wrong."

"Absolutely not," Nolan barked.

"It will help make all this go away and show you in a more positive light if they know what you've been dealing with. Also, you might want to mention where Heather's mother is."

Nolan stood and leaned over her desk, knuckles on the wood top, glowering. "I am not going to put my baby girl on display, nor will I discuss what happened to her mother. It's private, not to mention painful."

Jessica understood Nolan's need to exert his

power and desire to protect what he holds dear, but his stubbornness was going to make things worse. She leaned back in her chair and stared into the deep-green eyes of a hurting man. "Like I said, the slanderous statements we can kill with the truth. But the fact that not a single person knew you had a daughter, who has a problem that no one knows about, makes you look like a man who's ashamed of his daughter, and that is just as bad, if not worse in some ways. The press will have a field day with you about that forever."

"Is that what you believe? That I'm ashamed of my baby girl?" He leaned in closer. His nostrils flared. "Come on, Jessica. Tell me. No, I dare you to tell me."

She jutted her chin. "You want to play that game. Fine. I'd be lying if it didn't cross my mind." She pointed to her door. "And everyone else is out there thinking the same thing, wondering what other deep dark secrets Nolan Greer has. You want to shut this down and get the press off your ass? Then be a man and show them you're only trying to protect your pride and joy."

He opened his mouth but then slammed it shut, holding her gaze.

A long awkward moment followed.

"Nolan," she said softly. "Sit down. We've got a little bit of time, and I can push back the PR team and spokesperson for a little bit. Tell me about your daughter and why you felt it best for her to keep her hidden, and I'll tell you what I think you should put out there so we can protect your reputation, career, the team's, but also and more importantly, your daughter and family."

He closed his eyes, his chest rising and falling as he breathed so deeply it could be heard a mile away.

"Heather's mother died two years ago." Nolan blinked, his eyes moist with tears. He turned, leaning against her desk, his back toward her.

"I didn't even know I was a father until she called me on her deathbed. We barely knew each other. Dated for all of two weeks, then never spoke to each other for nearly two years. I was stunned. Didn't want to believe it, but every time I looked in Heather's eyes, I felt the connection."

"Did you—"

He raised his hand. "This is not an interview, so don't interrupt me or ask a single question. I tell this my way."

"Understood."

"Gina, Heather's mother, was a diabetic and having a child after having a kidney transplant is probably what killed her, a guilt I'll carry for the rest of my life."

Jessica wanted to reach out and put her arms around Nolan. Hold him tight. But he'd probably fling her across the room, considering how harshly she, and the rest of the world, had judged him.

"Heather had been born with a hip deformity that will probably never be completely corrected, but we've come a long way. When I first met her, she'd yet to have the first surgery because her mother had been so sick and had very little family. Heather could barely crawl at a year old, and without surgery, she'd probably never walk. Broke my heart, but before I took on the role of full-time dad, I needed to know for sure. We did all the paternity tests in a different state. I was living up north, and my career was iffy at best with the injury, so once her mother died and I knew she was mine, I moved back home. Around the same time, my mother was diagnosed. I didn't tell the world because I didn't want to make a spectacle of my kid or my mother's illness. The news about my injury and retirement had been a media circus, and I wanted to quietly accept this job and have a fresh start."

He wiped his face with both hands before

turning to face her. The contradiction of sadness and joy filled his eyes.

"The press hounded me right after the injury, and they all thought I went underground, which I did, but for my daughter. I let everyone believe I couldn't face my injury when in reality, I was trying to get to know my daughter. I never meant to keep her a secret. I'm certainly not ashamed of her, but I don't talk about her because..." he paused, letting out a long breath.

Jessica leaned forward, placing a trembling hand on his biceps, but he shrugged it off. Recoiling, she pushed herself farther from the desk, folding her arms.

"When Heather first came into my life, she had no idea who I was. Do you have any idea how hard it is to deal with something like that? My daughter, who needed a complicated and dangerous surgery, and I was barely able to comfort her because she was having a hard time understanding I was her dad, and all she wanted was her mommy, who had just died."

Jessica found herself taking in short, tight breaths, fighting her own tears. She understood him and why he'd kept his private life so private. She'd probably do the same thing in his shoes.

"I can't imagine," she whispered. "It's been a rough couple of years for you, and I get it, I do, but now we have to deal with the problem, and I think I have the solution if you're ready to hear it." The words sounded crass, but he'd pushed her away when she offered support. What little she knew of the real Nolan Greer, she knew to back away when any part of his body had a smidgen of anger.

He shook his head and chuckled, though it sounded more like sarcasm laced with a stick of dynamite. "Go ahead."

"We focus on the why. Simply stated: You didn't think it would be good for your developing relationship with her, and you were concerned about her long-term recovery, and you didn't want it done under the scrutiny of the public eye."

"When you put it that way, it doesn't sound so bad."

Jessica heard footsteps coming down the hallway.

"We'll work with the team, write a statement that you can give. We can make it a no-questions press conference, and then you can go home."

"What about the images of us kissing? What do I say about that?"

She swallowed her breath. While she didn't like

having her private life tossed under the bus, it wasn't important in the grand scheme of things. "Nothing. No one cares. A few comments trying to say you care more about a blonde bimbo than your kid, but that thread is long dead."

"If I'm asked?"

She shrugged. What was there to say? She certainly had a preference to how he handled it, though she would not tell him what to do. "Say whatever you want, but I doubt you'll be asked. If you are, you don't have to answer."

"I could tell them you basically assaulted me to make your ex jealous," he said with a dark tone, the kind intended to hurt. "The one who cheated on his wife with you."

She forced herself to maintain eye contact, even though she wanted to lower her head in shame. "You could and there'd be nothing I could do about it since it's a true statement. Go right ahead if you need to hurt me so badly."

"Maybe I should, so you know exactly how this feels."

6

The only thing worse than a press conference was having a catheter pulled out by a twenty-something intern.

Nolan looked around the crowd of people who'd gathered. Cameras clicked rapidly in the background. Reporters shouted questions at the team's spokesperson, who chose to answer a few, then stepped away after introducing him.

Nolan stepped to the podium with the well-written speech from a team of highly trained experts. He scanned the area outside of the main doors to the stadium, searching for Jessica. He found her sitting off to the side on a concrete step, laptop out, tapping away. He'd been amazed by how she could handle so many social media feeds at once and still make intelligent observations and conversation with all the team's followers.

But that didn't change the fact that she'd judged him, and then after he poured his heart out, she went right into business mode.

Clearing his throat, he glanced down at the paper.

"It is sad that I have to stand up here and defend myself against accusations that come from speculation and gross neglect for finding the truth before turning a trip to the Urgent Care unit with my daughter, who fell in the backyard playing with her grandparents' dog, into something it isn't. To be very clear, I will take legal action if this continues. The facts have been presented on what happened, and it will end there."

He took a deep breath, glancing up at the reporters with their microphones. Flashes of light hit his eyes, making him blink. He fisted the paper he'd been reading from. The next part he had to do his way. Didn't matter how great the speech was, if he was ever going to get the press to see him as a loving father instead of man with a temper, the words would have to come from his heart.

"I'm going to go off-script here." He held up the wadded piece of paper. "The words on this page would do well enough to explain the situation with my daughter, but they aren't my words."

He swallowed. What the hell was he doing?

"I'm not ashamed of my beautiful little girl. She's the best thing that has ever happened to me, and I'd walk away from all this if I thought it was the right thing for her." He took a few deep breaths. Having tears sting his eyes during a press conference was not something he wanted to experience. "I didn't know that Heather, that's my daughter's name, existed until she was a year old. Her mother had just died, which is when I first met Heather."

A few reporters yelled, asking why Heather had been kept from him. The last thing he wanted to do was toss Gina under the bus. She had her reasons for keeping Heather from him, and while he didn't agree, they were hers, and she wasn't here to defend herself. "That is not my story to tell, and I want, out of respect for my daughter, her mother's memory to be honored with the respect she deserves."

The clicking of the cameras had stopped, and the front of the stadium became painfully quiet. God, he hated having this many eyes on him and being aware of them, something that didn't happen on the football field.

"My mother always told me to never judge

others, not only until you've walked a mile in their shoes, but also, you never know what quiet battle someone is living, and we all have one. My daughter lost her mother, met her father, who was a complete stranger, and needed a series of major surgeries to correct a birth defect. What would you have done in my shoes? Because I bet most of you would have done your best to spend every waking moment getting to know your child and helping them through some difficult times. I will not apologize for wanting to do that outside of the public eye."

The stunned crowd stared at him with questioning eyes. He had no idea if he'd accomplished anything and didn't care if he got fired for going off-script at this point. He said what he needed to, and he said it from his heart.

His mother would be proud. Right before the conference, he'd spoken to his dad, who gave him the green light and so did his mother.

"I would appreciate it if you could give me and my family some space. Not only do we have some challenges coming up with Heather's surgeries, but my mother is dying of cancer, a battle we don't want to become the center of attention."

There was a collective gasp from the crowd.

"I'm begging you to let these matters rest and

focus on my coaching, which might be more contro-versial anyway, considering my reputation as being a hothead on the field."

The crowd laughed, and pictures resumed.

"Thank you for your time," he said.

"Coach Greer," a voice from somewhere in the crowd yelled. "Thanks for clearing all that up. But what about the girl you've been seen with, Jessica Roads, director of social media for the team. Is she your girlfriend?"

He glanced in Jessica's direction, and she stared at him with an open mouth. He could really hurt her if wanted to, but this media circus wasn't her fault, and if he were being honest with himself, she had done a good job with regard to this story, and she did it with grace and style. Most of all, she didn't beg him to spin their kiss a certain way, knowing he could make her look bad.

However, that didn't change that she'd believed the worst of him.

"I shouldn't even dignify that with a response. My love life is none of your concern." Nolan didn't care that his tone came off as clipped, but by the way the publicist had glared at him, he figured he should change his attitude a little when it came to Jessica.

"But you've been seen out with her on two

different occasions, kissing," the same voice yelled. "Do you have time to coach, take care of a child with special needs, and date a girl like Jessica Roads?"

He gripped the podium, feeling the wood bend in his bare hands.

"Don't engage," someone whispered from behind him.

"It's been rumored that Jessica—"

"Stop right there." Nolan felt that snap in his brain that happened every time he wanted to take a ref and put his fist through his face. Not literally. Nolan wasn't a violent man physically, but he could tear you apart with words. "I will not let you trash someone else's reputation as you tried to trash mine based on any kind of rumor. Nor will I let you judge me or whomever I choose to date. The focus should be on my ability to coach the offense of this team and help take us to the playoffs. So, I ask once again, give my family, and my girlfriend, some space and concentrate on football. I'm sure my outbursts on the field will give you plenty to talk about." He held up his hand as more people shouted questions. "Thank you for coming." He stepped back, letting the publicist handle the rest, realizing he'd told everyone he and Jessica were indeed romantically involved.

He shouldn't have answered the question in the first place.

As the crowd disappeared, Nolan searched for Jessica, but she was nowhere to be found. He'd expected her to stick around and either read him the riot act for going off-script or give him shit for implying something that wasn't true.

He checked her office, and the door had been locked. He texted twice. No response. When he finally arrived at the parking lot, her car was still there.

Fuck. He'd forgotten to give her the keys.

He pulled out his phone and called.

Right to voicemail.

He texted again.

WHERE R U? *I have your keys...*

THE CAPTION THING with three dots indicated she was responding.

GOT A RIDE. *On phone with my mother. I'll get keys tomorrow.*

. . .

LIKE HELL YOU WILL. Not often did he overstep boundaries, but he needed to talk to her and tell her he'd been hurt, but also, he owed her an apology, and she was going to hear him out.

Tonight.

He pulled the keys out of his pocket and got in her car. Opening the glove box, he found her registration and address. He knew the area well. Not a bad section of town. Safe. The building she was in had been one he'd looked at, but he'd decided on a townhouse with a yard, hoping someday his daughter would be able to run and play. He smiled.

Pulling out of the parking lot, he called his father.

"Well, hello there. Nice way to handle that situation," his father said without saying the standard hello, something that always annoyed Nolan.

"Hopefully it will put an end to it, and I can get on with my job." His family had been super supportive his entire life, always giving their two cents but never forcing their values or opinions on him.

"Mom wants to know if you were planning on telling her about your new girlfriend."

Nolan groaned. His mother constantly worried about his single status, wanting him to settle down. He had, when Heather came into his life, but not the way his mother had hoped.

It would break her heart if he told her the dating game wasn't real.

"I've only been out with her a couple of times. I didn't like where that reporter was going with his questions, and the word girlfriend just kind of flew out."

His father laughed. "How does this Jessica woman feel about that?"

"I'm going to see her now, so we will find out soon enough." He half expected to be slapped, but considering the kiss...two kisses...he hoped maybe they could actually start dating for real, assuming the media left them alone.

Nolan's pulse increased as he turned down Jessica's street. Women never made him nervous. He'd always been able to get the ones he liked, not that he was a player, but he hadn't been much interested in a relationship during the height of his career. "I'm pulling into Jessica's now. I'm not going to make it home before bedtime."

"Perhaps you should tell her that," his father said.

"Before you put her on, how's Mom doing? Are you both okay with her battle being public now?"

"In our world, it has always been public. All our family, friends, co-workers, members of the church have known since Mom got sick."

"I'm just worried about the press being parked out in our street."

"I think you're worrying for nothing," his father said. "Here's your munchkin."

"Hi, Daddy!" Her little screechy voice filled his heart with joy. He couldn't imagine what it would be like not to have the privilege of being her dad. It humbled him in so many ways.

"Hey, sweetie, how goes things? Did you have a good day?"

"I helped Auntie Karen make cookies!"

"Oh, can't wait to have some when I get home." He pulled into the parking area, hitting the button on the visor, hoping that was how to get into Jessica's garage. The gate hummed and lifted. But he had no idea where her parking spot was. He pulled off to the side in case anyone needed to get by. He tried to never cut a conversation short with his baby girl.

"Can we watch your press confrance? I only got to see some of it."

He smiled at her pronunciation. "I'm sorry, but

Daddy has to work a little late tonight, and I might not make it home until after bed. But I'll wake you up early, and we can have breakfast just the two of us."

"Breakfast in bed?"

"Yep."

"Okay, Daddy. Love you!"

He loved how happy and easygoing she'd always been. Even after the first surgery, she had this way of cheering up everyone else around her when it was supposed to be the other way around. He tapped his chest. "I love you more."

He hung up and called Jessica.

Right to voicemail.

Once again, he'd have to text.

WHAT PARKING SPOT IS YOURS? *I'm in the garage with your car.*

HE WAITED a few moments until a text flashed on his screen.

. . .

WHAT? *You're here? 54 is the spot. You can leave the keys under the floor mat. I'll get them in a bit.*

NOPE. Not gonna happen. He parked the car and strode into her building.

Damn, this woman made him do crazy things.

7

For the last twenty-five minutes, Jessica's mother had gone from lecturing her on how a lady is supposed to act in public to wondering when the wedding would be.

"Mom. I've got to go."

"If you don't want to come home for a visit and bring your new man, perhaps Dad and I should come down."

Jessica rolled her eyes. "You're welcome anytime, but just know how much traveling I do when the season starts, and the first pregame is next week." Her parents had visited her once at the end of the last season, and all they did was beg her to move back home.

The buzzer rang.

"I've got company. Talk soon. Love you."

Before her mother started on another ramble, she hung up. She did that often, and it always caused a pang of guilt. Her mom, even with all her quirks, had always been there for Jessica. Her parents were good people with big hearts and always meant well, a sentiment that she constantly had to remind herself of when she got frustrated with her mother.

"Hello?" she said as she pressed the buzzer, wondering who on earth was stopping by.

"It's Nolan."

Her heart skipped a beat before her pulse raced out of control. She couldn't tell if the sudden adrenaline was because she was still pissed about how he treated her before the press conference or because of what he said during it.

"You didn't have to bring my car here, but thank you." She dropped her forehead to the wall, hoping he'd go away.

"You're welcome. Now can I please come up? I need to talk to you."

She could say she was busy, but that would be a lie, and since she was pissed over his lying through omission, it wouldn't be right.

And now he'd hand-delivered her car.

"Sure. Fifth floor, apartment 503. I'll leave door

open, so just come in." She'd loved his impromptu speech about his daughter, but she'd cringed the moment her name was tossed into the mix. She grabbed a bottle of red wine she'd opened yesterday, pouring herself a hearty glass, making sure she got a good gulp in before she heard the elevator doors ding.

The doors swished closed, and she heard his footsteps walking the ten feet down the hallway, then a quiet tap on the door.

"Jessica?" he called.

"Come in." What didn't he understand when she'd said the door would be open. She rolled her neck, trying to relax.

He held up her keys as he did his sexy swagger across her small family room. "I meant to give these to you before the press conference."

"You didn't have to bring my car all the way here." When she took the keys, her fingers touched his, and they both froze for a moment, staring at each other. "Do you need a ride somewhere?"

He released his hand and pointed to her glass of wine.

"Oh. This is my first drink, so I can drive."

"I'll Uber, but I was hoping I could get one of those?"

She laughed, pulling down a wine glass. "Yeah, sure." What the hell was she doing? Get the keys, then kick him out the door.

They clanked glasses, toasting to nothing. An awkward silence came over the room as he sat at the breakfast bar, staring at her with a stupid grin.

"What?" she asked, not hiding her annoyance.

"I'm sorry about how I treated you when the story broke. It threw me, and I needed someone to blame. I know you had nothing to do with it."

"You owe that same apology to Brad."

He nodded, still grinning, which more than annoyed her. Not to mention he started with his insane tirade in the privacy of her office and not his public declaration.

"He didn't deserve that any more than you deserved to be judged and called nasty, untrue names in public and have your character challenged," she said, doing her best to pretend the man in front of her did nothing to her mind, body, and soul.

His grin faded. "Did you really think I was ashamed of my daughter the night you met her? After seeing the way I am with her, and by the way, bitchy move to call an Uber and leave when we were getting an x-ray and subsequent cast. It wasn't easy to explain to Heather why my new girlfriend left without saying goodbye."

"Payback is a bitch." Her heart pounded heavily in her chest. The word girlfriend hung over her like a puffy cloud with the sun trying to peer through. It would either downpour in a second, or the sun would brighten the sky. She wanted the latter but figured it was the former.

"I had a family emergency that first night." He cocked his head, holding his wine glass near his mouth. "Answer my original question."

"I didn't want to believe it, but think about this from my perspective." She pressed her hip against the countertop, one arm folded across her middle, the other holding a nearly empty glass of wine, which was already going to her head. "The guy I thought I loved had been lying to me for way too long about being married, and that has done a number on my ability to trust not just men, but myself. So, the shock of finding out that you had a daughter, especially after being so open with me, and...well...those kisses that's been spread all over social media, it was a little much for me to handle in one night. And I did say goodbye; you just chose to believe I would stay. Sorry, I felt a little betrayed. I wondered why you'd share something so personal as your mother and not tell me about Heather. Would you have ever told me?"

"Yes." He set his glass down, then leaned back and folded his arms. He was as serious as the first time she'd met him, with the grim glare and tight lips. "That first night, when you jumped me at the bar, I had come because I knew you were going to be there."

She coughed, then sucked in air, coughing more. "What? Don't mess with me."

"It's the truth, but I never thought anything would happen. Then you kissed me, and I thought maybe I would ask you out."

"Wow. Up until that night, you'd been an ass to me."

"I'm an ass to everyone." He laughed. "I'm the youngest coach on this team, and I'm trying to gain the respect of the players. Being a tough read helps, I think."

"Still doesn't explain why you didn't tell me about your daughter." Mentally, she flicked her cheek like her mother used to do when she continued to be inquisitive, not letting people avoid answering questions that made them uncomfortable.

"I thought about telling you when I talked about

my mom, but then we jumped right into the interview, and you were taping it."

"And you didn't trust me." She bit her lip. What did it matter? They barely knew each other, and his reasons certainly made sense.

"Trust has nothing to do with it. We went from personal to being professional, and that's how I handle all interviews." He shook his head. "I don't regret protecting my family, but I do feel bad about how I treated you."

She nodded, letting her anger and frustration float out with each exhale. She had no right to be upset with him about anything but his harsh words, and he'd apologized.

"Also, I didn't mean to blurt out you're my girlfriend. That reporter really ticked me off when it appeared he was going to say something nasty about you."

She swallowed, clearing her mind of any hope she and Nolan could be anything other than friends. It was too complicated between his family life and the way the press was reacting, and she couldn't, no, wouldn't push him like that. "I didn't expect them to ask the question. Honestly, all the information we had and looking at the press' response to the story, our relationship or lack thereof seemed like yesterday's news. It does bother me that the reporter who asked the question is a gossip columnist and has a reputation for stirring up trouble."

"That's all you've got to say about that?" He set his glass down. Red wine sloshed to the top. "I just announced to the world that you're my girlfriend."

"I just spent the last twenty minutes on the phone with my mother trying to explain to her that we were not dating, but I gave up. She wants me to bring you home to meet her, or maybe she and my dad will fly down here."

"I'd love to meet your parents." He grinned like a little kid.

"I was petrified you'd tell the truth, and I think that would have sucked less than my mother asking if we'd get married here or at home."

His eyes went wide as he started coughing.

"I do think the relationship thing will die a quick and painless death," she said, needing to stop beating around the bush and get to the heart of the matter. "If we're not seen together, the talk and gossip will stop."

He sipped his wine, staring out the window. "I like you," he said so quietly she wondered if she'd heard him correctly. "I find myself thinking of you at the oddest times. I enjoy talking with you." He turned, his green eyes mesmerized her, making her stand perfectly still. "I like kissing you, but—"

She blinked, understanding what the 'but' meant and where he was headed with the conversation. She didn't really need a rundown of why he was rejecting her. "Forget about it. We got caught up in a couple of moments."

He shook his head. "Do you always interrupt people when they are speaking?"

"I don't need a laundry list of why it's not the right time for you when I have my own list."

He set his glass down and did that sexy saunter around the breakfast bar into the kitchen. He pressed his hand on the counter next to her hip, his eyes keeping their gazes locked. "What I was going to say is that I have very little time between trying to prove to this team I'm man enough for the job and helping to take care of my mom, so my dad gets a break. There is also my daughter, who is the most important thing in my life."

"That's a laundry—"

He pressed his long, thick finger over her lips. "I'm trying to tell you my time is limited, but I want to make time to be around you. Dates might have to be lunch at work. An occasional night out on the weekends after I put my daughter to bed, and it's possible I could have to cancel because of family obligations, but I do like you, and you're fun to be around."

She curled her fingers around his wrist, pulling his hand away from her lips with the intention of telling him he was sweet, but she didn't think it a prudent idea for them to date. Only, he didn't give her the chance as he cupped the back of her head, his fingers massaging her scalp. His lips brushed against hers like the wing of a feather in flight.

A wave of dizziness rolled through her body when he pushed against the counter. His other hand caressed her back, fingers kneading her burning muscles. He deepened the kiss, swirling his tongue around hers.

The voice in the back of her head told her to push him away. That it would be too complicated, and she'd end up getting hurt.

Again.

But the way he kissed, it was like being wrapped in a warm blanket on a cool evening, watching the stars dance over the ocean. His tongue touched every part of her mouth like an electrical current. She shivered as she rested her hands on his shoulders, letting him guide the rhythm of their bodies.

He jerked his head back, his palm on her cheek.

"Why don't we have our first date right now? I talked to my daughter, and since I wouldn't make it home before she went to bed, she and I have our own little date planned in the morning, so I have some time now."

"I don't know," she whispered, staring in his Caribbean Sea-like eyes. Her breath was raspy as she sucked air into her lugs, letting it out in a swoosh. He had a strong effect on her mind and body, and it took her a moment to bring herself out of the realm of desire. "You keep catching me off guard and these kisses...It's too complicated."

"Come on." He took the wine bottle and the glasses. "Have you eaten dinner?"

"No," she said, staring at him moving about her kitchen, pouring their drinks into solo cups. "I never said I'd go out with you."

He laughed. "I think that kiss did."

"You didn't give me a chance to answer." She touched her lips, still feeling the warm caress of his tongue. Her brain was trying to process his proposition and why he'd been able to render her speechless with a single kiss.

"You kissed me back." His smile grew wide as he held the bottle up in the air. "Let's go."

"Where are we going?"

"To the terrace. It's private. Other than any neighbors from the building, all that is around is the beautiful view of the water and some palm trees."

"How do you know about that?" The private terrace was for tenants only.

"Same way I know the restaurant down the street will deliver."

He waved his hand in front, and she led the way to the elevator and down to the back of the building. The humidity smacked her face like a hot washcloth the moment she opened the door. The sun had lowered in the sky, but there was still a good hour left of sunshine. She inhaled sharply through her nose, enjoying the fresh scent of blooming flowers.

"What do you want to eat?"

"Bacon cheeseburger, loaded, cooked medium, and fries."

"Girl after my own heart."

During the summer months, the terrace didn't get used very often because of the heat, and tonight not a single person sat at a table or the chairs in front of the river leading to the Intracoastal.

Nolan chose the love seat closest to the water.

Sitting so close to him, smelling his manly sent of pine and spice, made her body crave another kiss.

She shivered. Her body wanted so much more,

and if she were being completely honest with herself, dating him sounded like a splendid idea. Every man she'd ever dated had been relatively serious from the beginning.

"Dinner has been ordered." He shifted, stuffing his phone in his pocket, and raised his glass. "Cheers to new adventures."

She smiled, clinking plastic cups, before taking a sip, letting the full-body wine slowly drizzle down her throat. "This isn't a date. This is co-workers getting together after work."

"Have it your way."

She planned on it. "So, what's the big date with Heather?" Jessica didn't mind long silences. She enjoyed people who knew there was a time to sit and enjoy the world around them. However, she wanted to know about his relationship with his daughter. It was a side of him she had never expected.

"Breakfast in bed," he said, smiling. "On the nights I don't get to tuck her in, I wake her up early so we can spend some extra time together. I know it doesn't make up for time lost, but I think it helps."

"It's got to be hard being a single father. How do you manage?"

"Are you always in interview mode?" He looped his arm over the back of the seat, his fingers resting on her shoulder. "I have a lot of help from my family. My sister doesn't work, so she watches Heather when I'm at work and will also take her when I have to travel."

"Do you ever think of taking her on the road?" She cringed. "I'm sorry. Inquiring minds and all."

"It's okay. I reserve the right not to answer." He laughed. "Not this year and I'll probably miss a game or two because of her surgery." His eyes lit up when he talked of his little girl, except when he mentioned the surgery.

"But in the future, you'd take her? I bet she'd like that."

He lowered his chin. "Are we playing twenty questions? Because if we are, I've got one for you."

"Have at it." She smiled. Even as a little girl, she'd asked a million questions to everyone, and it drove her parents nuts.

"Did Lilliana really dare you to kiss the next man who walked through the door?"

No point in lying. "That would be a true statement." Butterflies floated across her belly, rising to her throat. "When I was little, I did almost anything my friends dared me to, and now it's a running joke."

"Does that mean you still often take a dare?" He waggled a brow.

"Depends, but sometimes, yes."

"Hmmmmm, so if I dared you to kiss me right now, you'd do it?"

"Is that a dare?" Her lips tugged into a big smile, and her insides turned to mush. Her brain, however, reminded her that taking a dare, generally speaking, could get her into trouble.

He nodded, grinning like a schoolboy.

She took a sip of wine but didn't swallow before leaning in and pressing her mouth hard against his, forcing his lips to part.

He gave a deep, throaty grown as she passed the wine from her to him. He swallowed, tangling his hand in her hair as he thrust his tongue deep in her mouth, swirling wildly. He tugged, forcing her head back as he kissed from her lips, to her cheek, the side of her neck, and finally landing on her earlobe.

Her body shivered as goosebumps covered her skin.

"That, sweetheart, was a dangerous move, but a tasty one."

She tilted her head, enjoying his hot breath in her ear. The man made her want to throw caution to the wind and jump in with both feet. "Don't dare me to do things then."

"I didn't dare you to share your wine." He chuckled. "But I do dare you to flash me."

She set her wine glass on the ground and sat up tall, looking around. Not a single soul in view. What the hell. You only live once. Besides, her bathing suit top covered less than the current bra keeping her breasts in their proper place. Snagging the hem of the shirt between her fingers, she raised her shirt over her face, then pulled it down less than a second later.

He blinked, his mouth open.

"Do that again, only when you raise your shirt, count to ten."

She patted his leg before getting her wine. "Not going to happen."

"Not even if I dare you?"

She shook her head, heat rising to her cheeks. If they had been in the privacy of her apartment, she might have considered it.

He groaned, pulling his phone out. "Our food is here."

She handed him her keys to the main lobby. "You go get it; I'll grab a table."

"Because it's so crowded." He kissed her cheek.

She watched him head toward the building in that sexy groove where his hips swayed back and forth and you could see his back muscles flex against his shirt. His body could only be described as a solid mass of muscle.

But that wasn't the only thing she appreciated about Nolan.

Did I really just flash him? She folded her arms, looking around. No boats on the water and the thick trees lining the other side of the Intracoastal, blocking the view into the townhouses, protected her from being seen in that direction. No way anyone saw her...but Nolan. Oy.

An older couple followed him out of the building. He helped them carry their own little picnic basket and set it on a table for them, smiling and chatting for a few minutes before sitting down across from her at the table, opening two large containers of food.

The smell of grilled beef and crisp bacon filled her nostrils. Her stomach growled. "Thanks. I'm starving." She didn't wait another second, digging into the thick French fries which were soft on the inside but crunchy on the outside. Food was also a nice distraction from the hot man sitting across the table. Her toes itched to fondle his calf muscles.

"So, where do you live?" she asked.

"Here we go with all the questions again." He winked.

She cocked her head. "You know where I live..." She squinted her eyes. "How did you know that?"

"I looked at your registration card in the glovebox."

"That's creepy." She winked, enjoying the banter a little too much.

"You didn't leave me much choice when you disappeared."

"I'll give you that, but I feel like you're avoiding the question."

He laughed. "Right now, Heather and I are staying at my folks in South Beach, but I have a townhouse about two miles from here, a little closer to the ocean. I actually looked into buying in this building but decided I wanted a private backyard for Heather to play in. Do you rent here or own?"

"Can't afford to buy anything just yet. The rent isn't too bad, but I won't stay in this building when this lease is up."

He arched a brow. "Going to move north? Home?"

"No." She smiled. "I love my job and have no desire to do anything else right now. Besides, I like living in Miami."

"I hated growing up here but moving back has been a good thing for me." He wiped his hands with a napkin, tossing it back in the container and closing it. "Even better for Heather. A fresh start for the both of us."

A few more residents came outside to enjoy the sunset. She hadn't gotten to know many of the neighbors, but a few she recognized and waved. She picked at her food before closing the lid. The evening would come to an end soon. He needed to get home to his little girl. Being overcome by lust wouldn't serve either one of them very well. She didn't know if she wanted him so badly because it had been a while and he showed interest. Or the fact she just unequivocally wanted him in the most primal way.

"That was delicious," she said. The sky turned a dark blue, with orange and red swirls at the horizon. Soon the stars and the moon would glow like fireflies. She reached for the bottle of wine, but sadly it was empty. "Don't know about you, but I'd like one more glass."

"If I get to take it from your mouth again, sure." He reached across the table, taking her hand. His thumb rubbed the top of her hand in a circular motion.

"Maybe we should try it the other way around." Ugh. She really needed to think before she spoke.

"I'm game." He stood, collecting all the trash. "Let's go."

"I was kidding."

"I wasn't."

His enthusiasm gave her a tingle up her spine. His hand on the small of her back sent signals to the rest of her body.

Signals she needed to shut down, but her brain didn't work as fast as her body.

He opened the door to the building, and the cool air covered her skin like an ice cube melting over her body. The elevator opened, and they made their way to her apartment where he found a bottle of wine that met his fancy.

She handed him the corkscrew and watched his magnificent arm muscles twitch as he removed the cork, pouring a tiny bit into one glass.

He smiled, leaning against the counter, swirling the red liquid and smelling it. He waggled his finger in the come-hither motion.

Her breath hitched. He was actually going to feed her wine, and in her mind, that could only lead to one thing.

More kissing.

Kissing never hurt anyone.

He lifted the glass to his lips, emptying it, his other hand reaching for hers.

The soft touch of his fingers against her skin felt like the finest lotion money could buy. She tilted her head, pressing her body against his hard chest, staring into his intense green eyes. She told herself she'd be able to control her desire. Considering his situation, he wasn't the kind of man who jumped into bed with a woman without getting to know her better.

Interviewing him didn't constitute getting to know him.

He pried open her mouth with his tongue, shooting the warm liquid between her lips. She swallowed quickly, wrapping her arms around his shoulders and thrusting her tongue into his mouth.

She heard him set the wine glass down, then he wrapped his arms around her waist, spreading his legs and cupping her ass, drawing her even closer.

He kissed her so hard, she wondered if he'd bruised her lips. She almost hoped he did. The raw passion sizzling between their bodies controlled her mind, and she visualized taking him by the hand, leading him to her bedroom, ditching their clothes in a frenzy of desire, and having the kind of mad passionate sex one fantasized about. The kind where there were no inhibitions in the search to understand what pleased the other.

His hands glided up under her shirt, his fingers dancing across her bare skin. A tiny voice in the back of her mind whispered to stop, but her body screamed go for it. Wetness filled her panties, then she felt her bra loosen as he magically unhooked the clasp, moving his hands under her arms, touching the sides of her breasts.

"I dare you to flash me now," he whispered, breaking off the kiss, his breath raspy.

"Don't dare me unless you're willing to suffer the consequences, and the way things are going right now, how I'm feeling, I'm not going to be able to stop myself."

"I might be able to stop, but I won't promise."

She groaned as he ran his tongue over her earlobe. Her nipples tightened into hard little nubs. Taking a step back, she reached inside her shirt and pulled her bra through the sleeve. Her heart pounded against her chest. Doing this would either backfire, and he'd have second thoughts and she'd feel rejected. Or they'd end up tangled in her sheets. If the latter happened, a different set of complications would arise.

His gaze went from her eyes to her chest as he carefully poured himself some more wine, taking a large gulp.

Her fingers trembled as she toyed with the bottom of her shirt. She'd done a few crazy dares, like dropping her bathing suit in the pool and running to the house naked. Of course, that was with all her girlfriends and not a single male to be found. Sucking in a breath, she closed her eyes and lifted her shirt, focusing on counting and not the idea that a sexy man stared at her tits.

One, two, three, four, five, six, seven, eight, nine, ten.

Letting out her breath in a slow exhale, she lowered her shirt, blinking open her eyes.

Nolan stood in front of her with a wine glass in his hand, his lips parted, and his green eyes wide, still staring at her chest. "You're...that was...oh, fuck it." He yanked her hard against him, between his legs. His erection pressed against her lower abdomen. He kissed her in one of those sloppy, wet kisses that could only lead to one place, and she wasn't about to say no.

But she should.

His hands glided down her ass to the back of her thighs. He hoisted her up, wrapping her legs around his waist. "Where's your bedroom?"

"Down the hall, last door on the left. Condoms in the nightstand."

He jerked his head back, scrunching his face.

"That is why you were taking me to the bedroom, right?" She didn't blush often, but heat filled her cheeks.

He nodded. "Interesting that you didn't think I'd have any."

"Do you?" She smiled.

"No, but why do you have them?" He arched a brow.

"Leftovers. Sorry if that killed the mood."

"With the vision of your beautiful breasts ingrained on my brain for life, not much could destroy this mood." He lowered her body a little, his hard cock pressing against the very thing that made her a woman.

"Then why are we still standing here?"

He groaned, stumbling down the hallway, kicking back her door before tossing her on the bed.

"Nolan?"

"What, babe?"

"Before we go any further, this doesn't mean we're dating." Talk about killing the mood, but she needed to lay down the ground rules.

"It doesn't mean we're not." He stood at the end of the bed, hands on his hips. "What do you want?"

"I want you, but I want you with no strings attached. You have a lot going on, and I don't want to—"

"Fine. No strings." He lifted his shirt, pulled it off, and tossed it to the floor. "We good? Can I continue?"

She scooted back, propping herself up on a pillow. Not a single hair lined his tight chest. His pecs were perfectly formed, and all she could think about was kneeling in front of him so she could toy with his nipples. "Yeah. We're good."

He undid his pants and rolled them over his hips, down his long, lean muscles, showing off a pair of athletic underpants with the tip of his cock popping out of the top.

She bit down on her lower lip as he eased himself closer.

"Which nightstand?"

Leaning across the bed, she opened the drawer, fumbling inside until her fingers found what she'd been looking for, pulling out one and placing it on the top of the table.

"Sit up," he said with a throaty growl. He pulled off her shirt, letting his fingers rub against the swell of her breasts. He stared for a moment, licking his lips before averting his gaze to her eyes.

Her breath hitched as he traced a path from her lips, over her chin, stopping at her nonexistent cleavage. Lowering his head, he brought her tight nipple into his mouth, sucking deeply.

"Oh...my...God..." She stared down at him devouring her breast with his mouth, his hands fumbling with her slacks. She thought about helping him, but currently she enjoyed cupping his head and watching him while he sucked, nibbled, and licked at her nipple.

His fingers made their way inside her pants and panties, rolling over her wet clit, stroking it tenderly. He slipped a finger inside her.

"Oh..." She tossed her head back, grinding her hips, her clit throbbing out of desperation. Normally, she'd prefer a whole lot of foreplay, but right now, all she wanted was release. She lay back, helping him to wiggle her out of the rest of her clothing, her body now completely exposed. The light from the fan above shined down on them like a bright flashlight in the night.

He held her foot in his hand as he kissed her ankle, moving his way up her calf, the inside of her thigh before gently flicking his tongue against her throbbing clit.

"Ohhhh...ummm..." She moaned, clutching his head and letting her knees drop to the sides. His deft fingers entered her while his mouth made her body pulse with heat. Rising up on elbow, she looked down at him, his tongue swirling around. She'd watched a man pleasure her before, but Nolan did more than make her body feel good; he lit it on fire.

She tried to wiggle sideways, reaching for him. Needing to feel his hardness in her hands. Her hips grinding against his mouth and fingers. Pausing, he looked up at her and smiled.

"Wait your turn," he whispered.

Gasping for air, her stomach quivered. She clutched the sheets as he continued to torture her body. "Yes." She tossed her head back, rocking her hips faster, no longer wanting to savor the sensation. "Oh, God..." Wetness poured out of her body like hot lava flowing down the sides of a volcano.

His groan vibrated against her hard nub. She clenched her insides around his fingers as electric pulses jabbed at her womanhood. She convulsed so hard, it forced her to sit up. Clutching his head with both hands, her body jerked over and over again.

Her orgasm continued as he kissed the inside of her thigh.

With tiny tremors erupting inside her, she shifted her body. "I need to touch you."

He let out a small chuckle as he rolled to his back, slipping off his underwear. "I dare you."

"Normally, I'd say don't dare me, but in this case?" She stared at him for a moment in awe of his size, both length and girth. She ran her fingers across his lower stomach, her thumb brushing the tip of his cock. She swallowed, taking it in her hands, tracing the veins. She'd always enjoyed oral sex, but she'd never wanted to study a man before; then again, she'd never seen anyone as big as Nolan.

He ran his fingers through her hair but didn't push her, and that made the entire encounter even hotter.

Lowering her head, she licked the tip, circling it with her tongue.

He hissed.

Knowing she'd never be able to take more than half of him in her mouth, she stroked him with her hand and licked and sucked the tip. His skin was soft as silk. A nice contrast to the hardness. She'd never felt so sexy before. When she glanced up, he looked at her intently. His green eyes glossed over with desire.

For her.

She squeezed him harder, taking as much as she could in her mouth.

"Oh, Christ." His body tightened as she moved up and down his length. "Come here."

She kissed a path from his taut stomach to his lips.

"Do I need to dare you?" He reached for the condom, tearing it open with his teeth.

"I think you just did, and I'm up for the challenge."

He smiled. "Crazy question, but what position will make you come the quickest and hardest? You're all-time favorite position."

"No one has ever asked me that." Her body, already flush from desire, turned burning-building hot. She straddled him, her swollen nub over his hardness, slowly grinding.

"Or." She bit down on her lower lip.

"This right here isn't your favorite position, is it?"

She shook her head.

Sitting up, he kissed her neck just under her earlobe. His fingers massaging her ass. "Tell me, please."

"Tell me yours."

He smiled. "Not to be crass, but I'm a guy. They all do it for me."

Swallowing her breath, she moved her hips slowly over him. "Why don't I show you?"

"I like the sound of that."

She knew it was silly to be nervous about having sex a certain way. She hadn't been overly shy in the bedroom before, but since this was going to be a one and done, she wanted it to be memorable, not only for her...but for him.

Easing herself off him, she stood at the side of the bed, holding his hands, coaxing him to join her. She wrapped her arms around his shoulders, pressing her belly against his hardness.

He kissed her, his tongue teasing every crevice of her mouth, igniting a fire that burned through her body.

She turned her body so that her back was to him. His hands roamed her stomach and breasts, occasionally reaching down between her legs, caressing in slow, tortuous strokes.

"Climb on the bed on all fours," he whispered in her ear. "That's what you want, isn't?"

Every nerve ending in her body erupted like the finale fireworks on the 4th of July.

His hand glided down her spine as he gently pushed her toward the bed.

It amazed her how he could go from rough and out of control, to gentle and slow. His hands caressed her back and ass as she positioned herself. The anticipation both exciting and vulnerable.

He bent over her, his tip gliding against her throbbing nub, putting only the slightest pressure on where she needed him most. He kissed her back, shoulders, and neck. His hands reaching around her body, pulling at her nipples.

Dizzy with need, she pushed against him, feeling the tip enter her at just the right angle.

Slowly, he pushed a little more, then pulled out, repeating the motion until he was all the way inside her. His hands on her hips, squeezing tightly.

She fisted the sheets in her hands, pressing against him each time he entered her, clutching him as he pulled out. Her lungs burned as she sucked in deep breaths, letting them out in a giant moan. Their bodies rocked against each other like waves crashing into a breakwall. Slow and gentle at first, then erupting on impact.

His hands gripped her hips tighter as his rhythmic motion increased in speed and force. Without warning, he tangled his fingers in her hair, tugging. His other hand reached around her, pulling her up so she was just on her knees.

She gasped as he thrust himself inside, harder and faster. He moaned in her ear as he reached around and rubbed her clit vigorously, still pounding. The fan above hummed like a chopper as the blades cut through the bright light. Across the room she saw their tangled bodies in the vanity mirror, and so did he as they locked gazes. Stopping momentarily, he took her arms, looping them over her head and on his shoulders. His fingers danced across her body as if she were wet clay needing to be molded.

He moved inside her, staring at her eyes in the mirror. A dizzy haze filled her mind as the room continued to spin in pure delight. Nothing existed but their two bodies and the mirror.

"Oh, God," she cried out, feeling him expand inside her, and she shivered.

"Hmmmmm," he whispered in her ear. "That's it, babe."

For a second, she stopped breathing as an intense burn built from her nipples to where their bodies were joined.

He slammed into her with a loud grunt, holding himself deep inside. She felt his orgasm explode, and her body shivered as her climax burst through her entire body, shaking her in violent tremors. His arms so tight around her, intensifying the feeling because her body couldn't thrash about out of control.

His fingers still rubbed her, though softer and with less purpose. More of a tender stroke of one's arm by a lover's fingers while cuddling on the sofa, watching television. Then he pinched her, making her body shiver again.

"I think I might have a favorite position now," he whispered in her ear as he pinched her again.

Another quiver. "Oh, God." Her body continued to have aftershocks for the next few minutes as they gazed into each other's eyes.

He stepped away from her, pulling back the covers of her bed. She climbed under the sheets and watched him saunter across the foot of the bed toward the bathroom in his naked glory. Impossible not to stare.

Nor did he seem to mind.

He returned with a damp washcloth. Joining her in bed, he reached between her legs, pressing a cold cloth against her.

Her body gave one last little shudder.

"I'm experiencing the never-ending orgasm."

He laughed, drawing her in his arms, kissing her temple. "I could toy with your body all day long."

"I dare you," she said, smiling.

"Don't dare me," he said, running his hand up and down her arm. "Because if I ever do get to spend an entire day with you, it will be in bed, and I will find all sorts of ways to give you pleasure."

She draped her arm around his middle and rested her knee on his thigh. "You should have turned off the light before you got into bed."

"I can't fall asleep. I'm sorry. I really don't want to leave you, but I need to get to my parents' shortly."

Closing her eyes, she did her best to keep her breathing normal. She understood. But it didn't change the fact that it made her feel bad. Not cheap. Not used. Just bad, even if she'd been the one who wanted the no strings.

Nolan would always have his family.

8

*N*olan stood in the doorway to the room his daughter slept in, which used to be his room when he'd been a little boy. Pictures from various football-related accomplishments graced the walls, and many of his trophies were prominently displayed on shelves.

When he'd first moved in with his parents a month ago, the plan had been to have Heather stay in his sister's old room with its frilly décor, but Heather demanded to have her daddy's room. She'd stomped her foot, folding her arms and puckering her lips. No one could say no to that face.

Heather squirmed in her bed, her little face scrunched by her favorite teddy bear. The sun had yet to touch the morning sky. Part of him hated waking her, she looked so peaceful. But his heart ached to talk to her. Just him and his little girl.

He set the plate of pancakes on the nightstand and sat on the edge of the bed. "Hey, munchkin." He shook her shoulder gently.

Her eyes popped open. "Daddy!" She jumped up, throwing herself in his arms, knocking the side of his face with her pink cast. No greeting could ever be this good.

"I made us pancakes." He kissed her cheek, holding her tightly. Oftentimes, he resented that Gina kept his daughter from him for a year. He might not have loved her, or even liked her all that much, but he wouldn't have turned his back on her, or their daughter. But holding on to that anger wouldn't do him or Heather any good now.

She snuggled up next to him as he brought the plate of buttered pancakes to the bed. They always shared a plate. Five pancakes loaded with butter and syrup with two forks. "Do I get to see you on the television?"

He'd tossed and turned all night about whether or not that would be a good idea and based on the language and what the words implied, he opted it would be best if she didn't hear it. "Not this time. Some of the things the reporters asked aren't things little girls need to hear."

She looked up at him, brushing her curly locks from her face. "Because they didn't know about me? Or my leg?"

He coughed. "Where did you hear that?"

"I overheard Papa talking with Auntie Karen when I got up to use the bathroom. He said the reporter was rude and insen...insen..." She tapped her lips with her forefinger.

"Insensitive?"

"That's the word." She smiled, stuffing a large bite into her tiny little mouth. "Mmmmmm." She waved her fork in the air.

Heather could reduce him to a puddle of raw emotions in two seconds flat. He'd do anything for her.

Anything.

"I'm very proud of you," he said, fiddling with the fork. "I love you very much, and you know that my job sometimes puts me in the public eye."

She nodded. "You made the front page last week!"

He laughed. "I don't like being the center of attention, nor do I like my family being there. Just remember that no matter what, the things I do are to protect you."

"I know." She continued to dig into the pancakes. The girl had a healthy appetite.

They sat in the bed for another ten minutes, finishing the entire plate. She told him about the night before, and the story Grandmamma had read.

His mother waffled between having some energy to sit up and have conversations to being so weak she could barely eat. Her pain level increased so high they had to put her on medication. The doctors told them if she lasted the month, it would be a miracle.

"Will you be home tonight for dinner?" Heather asked.

"I plan to be." He batted her nose. "Maybe we can go out for ice cream after."

"Yay!" She wrapped her arms around him. "Daddy, is Jessica your girlfriend?"

"What gave you that idea?" His daughter had ears like a hawk and eyes in the back of her head. Nothing got by his little girl.

"Grandmamma said it was about time you had one when Papa mentioned the girl on the news was the girl who was with us when I broke my arm."

He pinched the bridge of his nose. He certainty didn't regret going to bed with Jessica, but the plan had been to have dinner, maybe a kiss or two, and plan a date for another day. "She's a friend that happens to be a girl." Besides, Jessica was the one that wanted a no-strings-attached romp in the sack.

"Can she come with us for ice cream?" Heather looked up at him with her bright-blue eyes, pleading. Her life had been far from normal. Shortly after she'd been born, her mother started to deteriorate. Heather had been taken care of by friends and family, all while her mother slowly died right before her eyes. It wasn't that Gina didn't want her daughter to have the surgeries, but she'd barely been able to take care of herself.

The last time he'd seen Gina before she died, he promised he'd do whatever it took to give Heather a good, happy life.

"I can ask her, but I can't promise she will be able to." Then again, it was Friday, so maybe she didn't have any plans.

No-strings-attached ice cream.

Heather nodded, her curly hair bouncing up and down.

"Let's go downstairs. Daddy made a big mess, so I could use some help."

He lifted her up. "You're getting too big for Daddy to carry."

She mushed his face, puckering his lips. "I don't need to be carried." She pressed her forehead against his, staring at him with a look of determination. Even when she'd been in physical therapy, in pain, she wore that look with pride. He wished he had half her resolve.

He laughed, setting her down. "All right, big girl. Let's go do the dishes."

Heather made her way downstairs while he gathered up his backpack with his computer and a few other things he needed for the day. He'd have a cup a coffee and visit with his mother and daughter for a bit longer, then head into work. His heart skipped a beat thinking about seeing Jessica and her beautiful smile. Somehow, he'd have to figure out how to manage a new career, being a father, and dating a woman who clearly, he had stronger feelings for than he wanted to admit.

With a spring in his step, he made his way down the stairs, where he saw his father standing at the front door, shaking his head.

"What's up, Dad?"

"I don't know, but there's a news crew out front."

"Shit," Nolan mumbled. The last thing he needed was for his daughter to be plastered all over the news for a second day.

"Nolan!" his sister called. "Come to the family room."

He turned to see his daughter with a scowl. "Auntie Karen says I need to go upstairs."

"I bet Grandma would like a visitor," Nolan's father said.

Just as Nolan bent over to kiss Heather, his phone buzzed.

He headed toward the family room, checking his phone, seeing a couple texts from Jessica.

DID you see the morning tabloid news program? WTH? They have a pic of me...well, outside. And they dug up crap from my past.

HE PAUSED MID-STEP, scrolling to the next text.

CALL ME. I'm sorry.

"SORRY FOR WHAT?" he mumbled as he turned the corner into the family room, quickly texting her back.

. . .

WE'LL TALK LATER... I

HE HIT SEND by accident when he saw his sister. He made a mental note to finish the text shortly.

"WATCH THIS," his sister said as she clicked the television remote.

"Jessica Roads, the social media director for the Miami Wildcats, recently linked romantically to the offensive coordinator, Coach Nolan Greer, was spotted with Coach Greer in the backyard of her apartment building. We had to black out most of the image as it appears Miss Roads flashed him." Behind the newscaster, a picture of him kissing her lit up the screen, followed by the now infamous flash. "Yesterday, Coach Greer made a statement about his young daughter. Considering this isn't the first time Miss Roads had bared all..." Another picture of Jessica, arms over her head, with five other women, all shirtless, popped up on the screen.

"Shit," Nolan muttered, stuffing his cell in his pocket.

"...at a woman's rally three years ago," the news-caster said.

"Shut it off," Nolan barked.

"I like this Jessica girl," Karen said. "I wouldn't have the nerve to do something like that at a protest, but I wish I did."

"I'm sure your Green Beret husband would love to see that happen, especially when he's deployed." His tone dripped with disdain.

Karen patted her large, pregnant belly, scowling. "Lighten up. It was for women's rights."

"Not when she flashed me, it wasn't." His phone vibrated in his pocket...and again...and again. "This is the last thing I need."

"Get over yourself. This isn't about you. It's about her." Karen pointed to the television. "She's the one who just had a big black line drawn over her boobs... twice." Karen held up two fingers. "You're just the doofus who sat there and stared at it with your mouth gaping open, like any hot-blooded male with a working penis."

Before he could say anything, Karen stomped out of the room.

He took in a deep breath. He knew the story was more about her, but still, he didn't need his offense distracted by his girl...by his friend...

Oh hell.

9

*J*essica stared at her phone as if to will him to text her, but nothing. The only time she'd heard from him had been at eight in the morning when he texted: *We'll talk later...I.* What the hell? He'd put her off like a ten-year-old who'd just spilled blackberry juice all over a brand-new white carpet. She tossed her phone on her desk and shoved her chair back, letting the rollers take her all the way to the wall, jerking her hard enough to give her the feeling of whiplash.

Asshole.

She stared at her closed office door. She'd been holed up in this room since nine in the morning, after being followed from her home to the stadium where she'd been accosted by a handful of reporters and photographers shouting at her. Her morning had been spent spinning the story about her being topless, which turned into an exercise of her poking fun at herself. But the image of her flashing Nolan? Putting a positive spin on that one had been difficult, and without any guidance from Nolan on which direction he'd prefer her to take, she had to make an executive decision and that was to move forward with the idea they were dating.

One tweet on her personal account that seemed to be catching on was:

IF UR NEW *bf dared you to flash him when no one was looking...would u? #newlove*

PEOPLE WERE TWEETING the crazy things they'd done to either impress someone or get someone's attention. She'd successfully pushed any attention from Nolan and who he should have around his daughter, and placed it right on herself, which was fine.

She also posted a few teasers from the interview with Nolan that would go live Monday morning, but she wanted to expand on the article, adding a few personal touches from Nolan. She knew he wouldn't like it much, but considering the stories circulating, she thought it prudent.

Except Nolan hadn't responded to a single text. She'd given up around two in the afternoon.

Now pushing six, she was still trying to get ahold of Derek Boyd, the photographer who took the images and the reporter, Greg Dugan, who worked for the tabloid show, but so far, neither one had responded. Not even when she'd tagged them in social media.

A tap at the door startled her. "Who is it?" she yelled. If it were Nolan, at this point, she'd tell him to screw himself.

"It's Lilliana."

"Come in."

Lilliana peeked her head in the door before stepping all the way through and closing it behind her. "How are you holding up?"

"I've been better, and Nolan is still ignoring me."

"From what I hear, he's having a tough time on the field. Lost his shit on one of the new, younger players who made some snide remark about you."

"That isn't helping."

Lilliana tossed a bunch of chocolates on the desk before sitting down. "I heard Alex Watson called him into his office."

"He called me in too. He said he'd fire Nolan before he'd fire me, but he's concerned about why this one tabloid is going after us. He believes they have either a beef with me, or Nolan."

"That's crazy."

"What's really nuts is I think it's me they are after. They really had to do some digging to get that picture of me at the rally. Only a handful of us had access to that image."

"Are your friends still pissed about their naked picture being plastered all over the news?"

Talk about the shit hitting the fan? That picture hadn't seen the light of day, other than by her and her friends. It wasn't meant to be a statement, but rather girls having fun at a march that had purpose. They'd promised never to share the picture with anyone. Had they been young and stupid, the snapshot wouldn't have been a big deal, but it had been taken as adults, each with careers that might view it negatively.

Jessica really didn't care that much about the image or the fact the world had seen it. But she did care about how it affected Nolan.

And his daughter.

"They have all taken it in stride since so far their

names have not been reported, but they aren't thrilled, that's for damn sure."

"I think the team spokesperson did a good job deflecting the situation, and it would appear you've managed to handle it on all the social media outlets." Lilliana leaned against the wall next to the door with a forced smile. "It's going to blow over."

Eventually, another scandal would catch the attention of the tabloid, and her flashing would become a distant memory in the eyes of the public. But at what cost?

"Want to come over tonight?"

Jessica shook her head. All she wanted to do was climb in bed with Netflix and a glass of wine. Binge-watch anything over the weekend, doing nothing but ignoring the outside world. Reboot and recharge. "Thanks, but I'm going to pass."

"Call me if you need me." Lilliana opened the door and gasped. "Oh, hello, Coach."

"Lilliana," Nolan's deep voice bounced off the walls, landing on Jessica's ears, causing a slight shudder.

"Finally decided to talk to me?" Slamming her laptop into her bag, she stood. "Well, right now, I've got nothing to say to you."

"I sense you're mad."

"No shit." She glared at him. "The moment the story broke, I texted you. I called you a few times, asking what you wanted me to do. How you wanted me to play this on social media, but noooooo, you couldn't answer."

His strong, wide body filled the doorframe. "I'm sorry, but I needed to focus on my job without this distraction. Besides, I did text you that we'd talk later, that I'd meet you here after practice and to handle this however you needed, and I would support you."

"On no, you didn't." She held up her phone, pulling the text up, shoving it in his face.

His eyes went wide. "I didn't finish the text."

"Consider me no longer a distraction. Now if you don't mind, I've got plans." Moving around her desk, she expected him to move, but instead he held his ground, his hands planted on his sexy hips. Her cheeks flushed as her mind danced with erotic images from the night before.

His musky scent filled her nostrils, and the way he looked at her reminded her of how his hands felt as they glided across her skin.

Lust. Pure lust. Nothing more.

"I'm sorry I ignored you. Between the news crew camped out in front of my parents' house, having to explain why they were there to a three-year-old, dealing with a few immature men on the field, and trying to get this offense ready for next weekend, I chose not to deal with it knowing you'd—"

"I don't want to hear it." She held up her hand. "You knew I'd need to do damage control for both of us, but you left me hanging. I had to make some decisions, and if you don't like them, too bad for you."

"I don't have any problems with how you handled it." He rubbed his jaw. "But I did tell you I didn't have a lot of time and that sometimes I'd need to focus on other things. I was running late this morning; otherwise, I would have stopped by earlier."

"Right. Well, we did decide no strings, but that doesn't mean you get to ignore me about a story that involves both of us just because you've got your panties in a wad." She narrowed her eyes, glowering at him. "Now please leave my office."

"No. We need to discuss something."

"And what would that be?" She should just shove him aside and storm out.

He pulled out his phone. "You mentioned in a text and voicemail about adding to my featured article or doing an entire series, making it more personal and letting people get to know me better and maybe that would help with the press hounding me."

"Right now, they aren't hounding you." She tossed her bag over her shoulder. "They seem to have a hard-on for me."

"Because you flashed me and—"

"Get out." She closed the gap between them and poked him in the chest. She couldn't blame him for her actions, but she didn't have to take his sarcasm.

"You really need to stop interrupting me." Holding her wrist, he stared at her with narrowed eyes. "It happened. We got caught. We move on. But I'm not willing to take that risk again."

She yanked her arm free. "Neither am I."

"Then we understand each other." The asshole had the nerve to crack a smile.

"Loud and clear," she muttered.

"Or maybe not," Nolan said as he rested his hand on her shoulder. "This isn't going as planned."

She cocked her head.

He dropped his hand.

"Okay, but you're still the social media director and I want to, carefully, ease my family life into the Dolphins organization, which means our fans as well. I want to do it in a way that will keep news crews off my front lawn, but also so I can take my kid to the grocery store without worrying my every move is being scrutinized."

"You're a celebrity, so to speak, so that's never going to happen." She stepped back from the powerful man, confused by how tender his touch had been moments ago, yet his words so hurtful. "We can easily change your image with a few pieces that candidly covers you and Heather and your journey to this place."

"I'd like to do that."

"I'll get someone in PR to conduct the interview. If you read all the texts, then you know the approach I want to take, which I believe will soften your image." Lowering her head, she took a step to the left, moving past him.

His fingers curled around her biceps. "No. I don't trust anyone else but you. Besides, it gives us some time together."

"Excuse me?" She blinked. "Why on earth would we want to spend time together?"

"I think you're mistaking my frustration over the situation and how I feel about—"

"Don't tell me what I think."

"If you'd let me complete one damn sentence, you'd hear me tell you that what happened doesn't change anything. I still want to get to know you better; it only changes how we go about it for now. Like no flashing in public. We date, but we don't give them any ammunition that could hurt either of us."

The way he stared into her eyes made her want to believe him, but his silence all day spoke volumes. Not to mention the way he'd brushed her under the rug out of convenience when a simple 'Got it, good with what you are doing, need to focus on coaching, see you soon' would have done the trick. "I can't date you. It's too complicated," she said. "But I'll do the interview. Lunch on Monday?" God, that sounded like a date.

He shook his head. "The article you wrote for Monday is really good and a great place to start, but it's standard. I've told that childhood story a dozen times over the years. I've mentioned wanting to be near my parents. But you didn't ask a single question about me. When I read some of your other posts from players and staff, they talk about life experiences. Things that shaped them. I want to follow up with something deeper."

"I'll keep that in mind. We can start Monday."

"Look, I'm not good at answering personal questions. I'm the master of generalities when it comes to interviews to keep me from flying off the handle, which is why I don't like doing them. I was thinking you could come over, see how Heather and I are together." He arched a brow as a slow smile drew across his lips. "People think I'm a hothead, which is true, but now they think I'm a coward. I know we did a good job of killing the accusations about me, but I'm still getting pinged as a man who is ashamed, and that is something I can't live with, nor have linger over the years, affecting my daughter. Heather's life is hard enough as it is."

"Can I see if Brad is available to take a few pictures of you and Heather?"

He closed his eyes for a few seconds before blinking them open. "Yes."

"When?" She'd make this the best damn series the fans had ever seen, and show the world the true Nolan Greer, but she and Nolan could never be a couple.

10

Saturday afternoon, Nolan stood behind the swing set in the backyard of his parents' house. Heather squealed in delight.

"Daddy, higher!"

Brad stood in the corner, taking pictures. Nolan tried to ignore him, acting as natural as possible, just as Jessica suggested, but he felt like a freak show. Thankfully, Heather seemed to be oblivious to the situation.

"If I push you any higher, you'll flip all the way around."

"That would be fun!" Heather giggled. "Do it!"

He laughed. "You'd fall out onto your pretty little head, and I'd think that would hurt."

"Okay. I'm thirsty."

Nolan grabbed the swing as it came toward his head, easing it down so Heather could do her best to jump off. She knew she had to be careful about jumping and running, but the doctor had also told Nolan that part of her ability to heal was her resilient personality, and he should do everything in his power not to squelch that.

"Why don't you ask our guests if they want anything as well?"

She nodded, her bouncy curls flying about her face. Nolan sat on top of the picnic table, watching Heather as she ran as fast as her brace and hobble would allow.

He smiled when Jessica gave Heather a fist bump.

"I'll get Auntie Karen to help with the drinks!"

Nolan nodded. "I'll take a soda."

As Heather disappeared into the house, Jessica rose from one of the lawn chairs and made her way across the yard. His fingers itched to pull out the elastic band holding her shiny blonde hair in a high ponytail. When she'd shown up earlier today, he tried to pull her in for a kiss, but she turned her cheek, something that didn't go unnoticed by his father or his sister.

He knew he royally screwed up by not calling her

yesterday morning. He could justify his reasons all day long, but the reality was he'd been scared and not just over the media making a spectacle out of his life.

No. He was scared of Jessica and the way she made him feel.

"She really is adorable." Jessica sat down next to him but kept a safe distance. "She has your eyes."

"She has my hair too." He glided his hand across the top, reminding him he desperately needed a haircut. "Not to mention my temper."

Being near Jessica made his heart beat a little faster. His skin tingled. His lips sizzled. But what really did him in was how his mind conjured up a future that included a woman...specifically...Jessica.

"You're a good father."

"Thank you." He adjusted his body so he could look at her. The sun beat down on her face, highlighting her tanned skin and pink lips. Her beauty took his breath away. "It's been a bumpy road to get to this point." Pressing his hands on the picnic table, he shifted closer. "You haven't recorded any of this."

"It's not an interview." She swirled her hair around her fingers. "I was thinking I'd rewrite Monday's article altogether. With the game coming up next weekend, it's important we do shift the focus back to the game, and I see no point in drawing out the attention on you and Heather."

"Will you be able to write that by Monday morning?"

"I believe so, but I'd need you to sign off on it by Sunday around dinnertime."

"I won't need to," he said, reaching for her hand. "I don't want to taint what you see after spending a few hours with us." A warmth spread through his body as he laced his fingers through hers.

"I don't want to say anything—"

Lifting his other hand, he pressed his forefinger over her lips. "I want you to write the truth about what you see here, nothing more, nothing less. I trust you."

The corner of her lips turned upward.

He cupped the back of her neck, massaging gently, pulling her closer. "I screwed up yesterday big time. I'm sorry."

"It's over," she whispered, her gaze darting from his eyes to his lips.

He smiled. "Have dinner with us tonight." Not wanting to hear her rejection, he parted her lips with his tongue, wrapping his around hers in a slow, twisting dance.

A soft moan trickled from her lips. He swallowed it as if it were the finest wine money could buy.

He eased closer, resting a hand on the small of her back, her body leaning toward him but not touching him. Without breaking off the kiss, he tugged her closer, pressing her chest against his, feeling her heart beat with his, making him dizzy.

The sound of the back door sliding open tickled his brain. He could hear a whisper coming from the house, but he ignored it, wanting to savor Jessica's taste. Hold her in his arms a little while longer.

"Shhhhh, Auntie Karen, don't interrupt; he's kissing her," his daughter said in a hushed tone.

Jessica stiffened, breaking off the kiss, breathing labored, trying to pull away.

He continued to hold her, his forehead pressed against hers, his eyes blinking open. "I think our drinks are here," he whispered before kissing her temple and releasing his grip.

Not letting her squirm too far away, he kept his arm looped around her waist.

"Here you go." His daughter handed Jessica a soda before climbing up on his lap.

Karen gave him a shitty grin as she handed him a can along with Brad.

Crap, he'd forgotten about Brad. He really hoped

he hadn't been in the corner snapping pictures of that kiss...he wiped his lips.

"Thanks for this," Brad said, holding up the can. "I've got more than enough pictures, so I'll excuse myself." He pressed something on his camera and handed it to Jessica. "Just give it back on Monday. Once you download the images, you can delete them from the card."

She nodded, slipping it into her phone case.

"Can I see the pictures?" Heather had lifted her bad leg, resting it on his knee. He knew she'd overdone it. She always did.

And she almost never complained.

"I'll send them to your dad, okay?" Jessica reached out, brushing back a lock of Heather's hair. "I bet there are some really great ones of you and your dad."

"Thanks for letting me take the pictures," Brad said, holding out his hands. "I'm not billing them to the team, so they are all yours. I think there are some really good ones that would blow up nicely."

"I appreciate it."

"I'll show you out," Karen said.

A long silence followed as Nolan eased his thumb between his daughter's brace and her hip, massaging gently. Her hip joint hurt her the most, but on days where she played hard, which was most days, her knee bothered her as well. Heather rested her head against his chest with her plump little hand under her cheek. Her other hand looped under his arm.

"I think someone is tired," he whispered, kissing the top of her head. She didn't nap often, but if she were to take a power nap, it would be just as dinner approached.

"No, I'm not." She yawned.

He chuckled as he glanced over the top of her head.

Jessica sipped her soda, looking around the yard, her gaze everywhere but on him. "I should get going too."

"You never answered my question about dinner." His daughter's breathing slowed as she drifted off into a peaceful sleep in his arms.

"I want to get started on the article."

"Look at me," he said softly.

Slowly, Jessica turned, her eyes locking with his. The corners of her mouth tipped upward. "Thanks for letting me into your world. I understand why you've done things the way you have, and I promise I will paint that picture."

"I know you will." He let out an exasperated sigh.

"Please stop avoiding the question. Heather was so disappointed when you didn't join us for ice cream last night. I told her I'd ask you tonight."

"Dairy Queen," Jessica's smiled brightened. "She's been asking me all afternoon."

"Really?" He tried to act surprised, but his little girl had his same determination and persistence.

"Listen. I've had a great time today." She reached out, running her fingers through Heather's hair. "But I've intruded enough on your family time."

"If not for me, then for this little girl. She likes you, and it would mean a lot to her."

"Resorting to using your daughter to get me to stay?"

If it weren't for the playful look in Jessica's eyes as she batted her lashes, he'd be insulted.

"When my kissing doesn't do it, and not to brag, but I'd say I'm a good kisser, then yes, I'd resort to just about anything." He winked. "Even daring you to join us."

"My daring days are over."

"That seriously bums me out because I have an entire list of things I'd like to dare you to do. One of which has to do with that pool over there."

"Shhhhhhh." Jessica held her finger over her lips. "Not appropriate talk in front of a toddler."

He leaned a little closer. "Come here," he whispered, placing a hand on her shoulder, coaxing her closer. "Please? I'm begging here." He kissed her softly. Her pouty lips were plump and moist.

"Okay," she said, pulling back. "But I have to leave right after. I really do need to start on the article if I'm going to get it done by Monday and have it be any good."

Looking into her eyes, his heart fluttered. He'd had a couple of long-term relationships and a few women he'd really cared about. But not a single one would he have ever begged to go out with him.

11

*J*essica had never been so nervous about an article before in her entire career. Before the Dolphins, she worked for a team management company, doing similar things, and before that, she wrote articles about sports for a local magazine.

But she'd never written anything so emotionally gripping before. She'd cried three times.

And then there were the pictures.

Brad had outdone himself.

Taking a deep breath, she opened her laptop, keying in her passcode, then pulled up the blog and the social media feeds. It had only been ten minutes since the post went live and already there were over thirty comments.

She clutched her chest as she read through them, smiling as they were all glowing. People related to him and his daughter and what they had gone through. One reporter even apologized for jumping on the 'gossip bandwagon.' A few more comments popped up as she scrolled down. All good...except one.

SW_DolphinsFan: This is a very touching story. Coach Greer and his daughter seem to have a special bond, and from all the other reports coming in, this appears to be a true picture of their life. However, I must comment on the author of the article, if she is indeed the author. I mean, it's so far off her normal posts. I mean just look at the language and style and compare it to previous articles. Makes me wonder if she didn't have someone else write it. Really, out of the woman's ability, and she's been known to do this before at her college paper, taking credit for someone else's hard work. Tsk. Tsk.

"Shit," she mumbled. The same poster tweeted the false accusation and posted the same comment on other social media outlets.

She looked up the account, only to find it had

been created this morning. Nothing worse than a fake account and a troll.

For the next hour, she focused on the article, not the comment or those who chose to reply to the negative comment that had no bearing on the article.

Don't feed the trolls. Generally, a good motto to live by on the internet.

She'd been able to bury it across all platforms until the fake poster stopped commenting on the thread and created a new one.

SW_DolphinsFan: People, we really need to stop allowing this woman to take credit for this. In no way did she write it. Compare the opening paragraph to this one from last week's feature.

The post linked her feature blog on the head coach.

I'm sure you intelligent folks out there can see the difference. We need to one: back away and stop commenting on this, giving her praise, and two: request she be removed from the organization. For all we know, the image of her flashing Coach Greer had been planned for her two minutes of fame. LET'S SHUT THIS DOWN, PEOPLE!

"Asshole." Don't feed the trolls, she continued to remind herself as she focused on posting other players' images, their stats, as well as who the fans could expect to see during the first preseason game.

Two hours ticked by before her stomach growled. Normally, before she'd grab a bite to eat, she'd check the feed again, but this time, she thought better of it. She hadn't heard from her superior or the head honcho, so she figured the troll was a faint echo in cyberspace.

A tap at the door startled her, and when she glanced up, she was surprised to see Nolan instead of Lilliana.

"Hungry?" he asked, holding up a take-out bag from the burger joint across the street.

"Actually, I am." She closed her laptop. She hadn't seen him since Saturday evening at his daughter's favorite restaurant. The only communication they'd had were a couple of text messages about the article with a couple flirty ones tossed in for good measure. "What'd you bring?"

"The only thing I've ever seen you eat."

She laughed. "I'm going to get fat hanging out with you." Pushing aside the papers on her desk, she made room for the two take-out trays. "Did you read the article?" She'd been worried all morning about what he might think of it. The negative poster was correct in one thing: it was a departure from her regular sports style.

"I did," he said as he sat down across from her, piling ketchup on his French fries.

"Before or after I posted it."

"I told you I didn't want to read it before it went up." He licked his fingers then tossed her a few packets. "It made for an amusing morning practice when I told one of the players that my daughter ran faster than he did."

She laughed. There seemed to be a lightness about him that hadn't been there before. "What did you think of the pictures?"

"I didn't realize how much Heather looked like me until that side-by-side picture of me as a baby and her."

She watched him bite into his burger. He made everything look sexy and desirable, and she no longer cared that he had little time for her because she understood how important his daughter was, and Jessica had no problem being second fiddle to that little girl. "Did you look at the ones I sent privately?"

He nodded. "I want to have a couple blown up. Give one to my dad for a Christmas present."

"Which one?"

"I sent an email to Brad with the ones I really liked and copied you on it."

"Oh. I haven't checked my email. Too busy floating posts for this weekend's game."

"I was glad to see you ignored that one asshole who decided to try to make trouble for you."

She swallowed then coughed, nearly choking on her hamburger.

"You okay?" He leapt from his chair, jumping around her desk, and smacking her on the back.

"Fine, really." She held up her hand. "Just caught off guard by the fact you read the comments."

He leaned against her desk, staring down at her. "One of the other coaches told me about it, so I checked it out. I was tempted to comment back, but I figured why add fuel to the fire and you ignored it, so...." He shrugged.

"I appreciate you thought about it and glad you didn't."

Eight days ago, she'd thought Nolan was an arrogant ass with a temper. He did have a temper, on the field, but off, he became a big softy with a kind and gentle soul.

He took one of her fries, then smothered it in some ketchup before offering it to her mouth. Heat spread through her body as he placed the treat on her tongue. She drew it in, taking the tip of his finger with it, sucking on it for a moment.

"I missed you yesterday." He traced her lips with his forefinger. "Starting this weekend, I'll have even less time to see you."

The warmth stirring in her body chilled.

Family first. He'd said those words a half-dozen times on Saturday, a concept she respected, which made this entire situation that much more difficult. She'd been a part-time woman to another man...a married man, who should have been putting his family first. Even though she hadn't known Robert was married, she'd always felt as though she came last in his life. That his career meant more to him than any person and her being the least important thing in his world.

She wanted to matter to someone, as selfish as that sounded; she wanted to be on the top rung on someone else's ladder.

Something she'd never have with Nolan because

he was a loving son and a dedicated father who put his family above all else.

The kind of man she wanted for herself.

"What's the matter?" he asked, his fingers gliding through her hair, pushing it over her shoulder. "You're scowling."

"Sorry," she said, her mind scrambling to come up with a reason for her sour mood that didn't make her look like a childish, selfish bitch who needed constant attention. "I think that comment on the blog bothered me more than I thought because there is one part of it that is fact."

"What's that?" He cupped her neck with his long fingers as his thumb gently rubbed her cheek.

Damn him for making her feel as if she were at the top of his ladder.

"My tone and style with your piece was a big departure from the way I normally write."

"Did you do that for a reason?"

She nodded. "It was an observational piece, not a recount of an interview. I tried to do it as an outsider looking in." Only, without realizing it until after she'd posted it, she'd layered in some of her personal feelings for the sexy coach and father.

"I don't know much about writing." He curled his fingers around her shoulders, pulling her up and easing her between his legs, his strong arms circling her waist. "But I really liked it, and I normally hate anything written about me. My mother wants to meet the woman who finally understands her son."

Jessica swallowed. The other day, his mother had been having a bad time and wasn't up for company, much less meeting anyone. Had Jessica known, she would have insisted that she and Brad come over another time, but her presence didn't seem to upset any balance. The house was filled with love and support, and even though she knew a dying woman rested somewhere on the second floor, life was being celebrated.

"I'm far from understanding you." She rested her hands on his shoulders, feeling the tight muscles constrict under her gentle massage.

"Can you come over after work and have dinner with us?" His hands glided between the small of her back and the top of her ass. His touch was filled with promises of ecstasy.

"I don't want to intrude on—"

"Please stop saying that." His arms gathered her tight, pressing her chest against his hard pecs.

Her breasts heaved against him with every deep breath. Her nipples were painfully erect and tight.

All he had to do was look at her, and she was putty in his hands.

"I want you there, and you're all Heather has been talking about." He winked. "She thinks it's important she gets to know any woman who kisses her daddy to make sure they are good enough."

Jessica tried to tear her gaze away, but his green eyes lured her in so deep, she found herself molding her mouth with his in a familiar slow dance, their tongues anticipating each other's next swirl.

"Have you ever had sex in your office before?" he whispered as he nibbled on her ear.

"Can't say that I have." Her words came out in one big pant. She thought about jumping up on the desk, dropping her pants, and letting him do whatever he wanted. "Don't have any protection and doors are not locked." She squeezed her eyes shut. Heat rushed to her cheeks.

"I can fix both those problems." He pushed her aside and ran to the door, slamming it shut.

Wetness poured out of her at the click of the lock. She throbbed when he tossed the condom on the desk.

"First time I've bought those in two years." His triumphant smile made her giggle. "Glad that amuses you." He stood in front of her, fingers toying with the button on her pants, gently gliding the zipper down.

She bit down on her lip as his hand glided across her stomach and into her panties, his middle finger sliding between her wet folds. Her pulse pounded in her ears like a conga drum. His warm lips kissed her neck just under her ear. "Remind me to wear skirts more often." She pushed her pants down over her hips, kicking off her shoes, and removing her slacks.

"It would make this easier." He continued to nibble on her neck, kissing his way to her cleavage, biting at her nipple through her shirt. She should care that he made a wet spot, but she didn't. His soft hair tingled her fingertips as she admired the way his lips heated every inch of her, wishing he'd removed her shirt.

Lifting her onto the desk, he sat in her chair, tossing her legs over his shoulders, forcing her back on her elbows. "Say you'll come over for dinner." His middle finger traced her opening in a gentle stroke.

She squirmed. The desire to be filled by him took over her body as she rocked her hips against his hand, trying to draw his finger inside her.

He kissed the inside of her thigh.

She dug her heels into his back, moaning, yet he barely touched her.

"Say it." His mouth and finger hovered over her like a hummingbird.

"Oh...please, Nolan."

He looked up at her with an arched brow. "Say you'll come to dinner, and I'll take care of this." His thumb grazed her clit, then his finger dipped inside her for a second before he pulled it out and brought it to his mouth. "Come to dinner tonight."

"This is blackmail."

He kissed her swollen nub. "It is and this is about all you'll get unless you agree." Puckering his lips, he blew on her.

"Oh...my...God. Fine. Yes. Dinner. Tonight."

He smiled.

The room spun as he wasted no time pleasing her with his mouth and tongue. He kissed and sucked with wild abandon. Her nerve endings exploded with every swirl of his tongue. She couldn't take her eyes off him and what he did to her body.

She fumbled with the buttons on her blouse. Her breasts demanded attention. Begged to be fondled. As soon as she unclasped her bra, she grabbed his hand and squeezed it over her breast.

Dropping her head back, she blinked. The bright florescent light flickered from the ceiling. She gripped the edge of her desk, heels digging into his shoulders, toes curling.

"Oh....God..." she ground out.

His thick fingers entered her as he kissed her stomach, making his way up to her exposed nipples. His hot, wet lips brushed against one, then the other, going back and forth as his fingers glided in, stopping and curling at the right moment before slipping out again.

"I have to have you." She clutched his head, pulling him from her breasts. "Now."

"Yes, ma'am," he said with a smile before ramming his tongue inside her mouth. This man kissed like there was no tomorrow. He stroked the inside of her mouth much the same way he'd done when his head had been between her legs.

He stepped back as he let his trousers fall off his hips.

"Beautiful," she whispered, watching him roll the condom over himself.

"I believe that is my line."

She pushed him, forcing him down on the chair, a little too forcefully, but he didn't seem to mind as his smile grew larger. His eyelids lowered and his light-green eyes turned dark and smoky as she slowly lowered herself over him, taking him inside her, inch by glorious inch.

He leaned back in the chair, hands gripping her hips, gaze locked on her hands toying with her breasts. She rolled her hips slowly, enjoying how difficult it seemed for him to remain in control. His fingers dug into her ass so hard they had to have left bruises.

The build-up started in her toes with the tingling of her skin. Her ankles heated, and the warmth crawled up her body like a hot burning match. She rubbed her nails against her nipples, grinding her hips a little harder and a little faster.

He smiled like a schoolboy as he leaned forward, sucking a hard nipple into his mouth, his hands cupping her ass, his hips moving against hers.

Her breaths came in quick pants. Her thighs ignited as if kerosene had been tossed on her flaming body.

"Oh...Nolan..." She moaned, clutching his shoulders as his hips jerked and his girth swelled inside her like a stick of dynamite about to explode. "Oh...."

Nolan nibbled his way up her neck, biting her lower lip. "Cum for me, Jessica."

Her body shivered as her stomach shuddered.

Tremors washed over her like the ocean waves rolling onto the beach. As soon as one shock retreated, another slammed against it, pushing it harder.

He grunted, thrusting himself deep, pushing her hips back and forth until he groaned so loud, whoever was in the conference room next door heard him. With his head buried in the crook of her neck, he continued to ease her hips over him until they both had a chance to catch their breath.

She held him for a long time, stroking his hair, massaging his neck, wondering how in eight days she had lost her heart.

$\mathcal{N}$olan walked out of Jessica's office, waffling between a smile and a scowl. Screwing her in her office had to be the most memorable sexual experience of his life. Only he wanted to think of it as making love to her. Could one fuck like there was no tomorrow and it be the same as lovemaking?

This struggle over how to qualify the romp on her desk tugged at his heart. He thought he had no room left in there for a woman, and yet there was Jessica. He found himself wanting to find ways to combine his home life with a love life, hence the invitation to dinner, which both his daughter and his mother constantly asked him to do.

But all that brought a smile to his face.

The scowl came from the fact the condom had broken. Brand-new pack and the damn thing broke. It wouldn't have been that big a deal since he trusted her to be honest about being clean, and he knew he was. Abstinence had all but guaranteed that. But when he told her what had happened, she replied with, "Fuck, I'm not on the pill."

Ever since Heather had entered his life, he never allowed himself to believe he'd marry or have any more children, which honestly hadn't been high on his list of things to do. But now he found himself entertaining both concepts, and that scared the shit out of him, mostly because of the way Jessica's face contorted at the prospect of being pregnant.

Not to mention they'd only known each other for a month and had been a couple, if one could call them that, for eight days.

He pulled into his parents' driveway and immediately knew something was wrong when he saw his sister and Heather in the yard, waiting for him. Karen's eyes were moist. Heather smiled and waved, but it wasn't her usual happy self.

"What's going on?" he asked as he stepped from the SUV.

Heather ran, as best she could run, arms flapping at her sides. "Daddy."

He scooped up Heather and squeezed her tight. She sniffled, burying her face in his neck. "Grandma is having a really bad day."

Ambulance, his sister mouthed.

The sound of tires churning up broken gravel stole his attention. Looking over his shoulder, he saw Jessica pull in. He pointed to the spot next to his SUV. "Heather. If Jessica is willing, how would you like to go get a burger and a shake?"

"Are you coming, Daddy?"

"No. I think Auntie Karen and I need to stay and help Papa."

"She's going to the hospital, isn't she?"

He closed his eyes. He didn't want the hospital to ever be a bad place for Heather, only a necessary evil in her journey to having a leg as good as it could be. While his mother had a do not resuscitate order along with no heroic measures, she didn't want to die at home. Her fear was that it would turn the family house into a constant reminder of pain and agony, and she didn't want her husband to feel as though he had to sell.

"She'll be more comfortable at the hospital," he whispered, stroking his daughter's curly locks.

"It's her time, isn't it?"

"I don't know, baby, but for now, I think it's best if

you let me and Grandpa worry about Grandma, and you go have some fun with Jessica."

"What kind of fun?" Jessica placed her hand on his shoulder. "Oh, Heather, what's wrong?"

"It's Grandma." Heather shifted, her arms lunging toward Jessica.

"Whoa," Jessica said as she grabbed the little girl who had flung herself.

Nolan scratched the back of his head. Heather had always been an outgoing little girl, but in times of need, she tended to cling to him. The doctor had said it was because she'd lost her mother so young and was forced to rely on him, a stranger at the time, through her first surgery and that they formed a parent/child relationship that in many ways was stronger than if he'd always been in her life.

"Daddy doesn't want me here when the amblewence comes."

It was impossible not to crack a slight smile over the way his daughter said some words. "I thought you two ladies might like a night out on the town alone."

Jessica nodded.

"Take my car." He pried Heather from Jessica's arms and eased her into the car seat. "You be a good girl for Jessica, okay?"

"Yes, Daddy." She puckered her little lips for a kiss, and he didn't hesitate.

"I love you." He closed the door, handing Jessica the keys. "Are you sure you don't mind?"

"We'll be fine." She squeezed his biceps. "Take care of your mom."

"The keys to the house on are on the ring or take her back to your place. I don't know how long I'm going to be, but I promise if it gets to be past ten, I'll come get her."

"Don't worry about it."

He leaned in and kissed Jessica's cheek. "Thank you," he whispered.

Sirens blipped in the background.

Nolan tapped his chest as he watched Jessica pull out of the driveway with his daughter safely tucked in the back seat.

His sister patted his shoulder. "Little brother, you are head over heels in love with that woman."

The next couple of hours went by in a blur. Doctors and nurses came and went as his mother faded in and out of consciousness. His sister's husband had managed to Skype from his deployment in the Middle East to say his goodbyes. Nolan understood why he didn't rush home, saving his time so he could make it back in time for the birth of his first child.

Something that had been robbed of Nolan by Gina. He was no longer bitter, but there'd always be a pang of anger over the stolen moment.

The hardest part of the evening had been when the priest had come by to read his mother her last rites. Shortly after, she'd drifted off into a deep sleep. Thirty minutes later, his mother was dead.

He sat in the waiting room, his face in his hands, tears burning his cheeks. No matter how prepared one was for death, when it came, you realized you can never prepare. He'd called Jessica and told her the tragic news, asking her not to say anything to Heather. He needed to be the one to tell her.

It had been a difficult decision to move into his parents' house with Heather, not wanting to fill her little life with doom and gloom, but she'd brought such joy to his mother that he couldn't deny a dying woman's wish.

So, what was he supposed to do with his mother's engagement ring? He dug into his pocket, pulling out the large diamond. Before the paramedics had loaded her into the ambulance, she'd handed it to him, telling him that she knew without a doubt that he loved Jessica.

Eight days, and he'd lost his heart.

His mother was right. He loved her. But was he ready to make a commitment to her and more importantly, was Heather?

He leaned back in the chair, glancing down the hallway where he saw a woman standing sideways, hand on her pregnant belly. His chest swelled with a mix of love and fear. Like his daughter, he couldn't imagine spending a single day of his life without Jessica in it. He shook his head. If he declared his love for her, she'd think he was nuts. Not only that, she'd probably think it was because of the broken condom.

Which scared him on a different level because part of him hoped he'd gotten her pregnant, which was beyond nuts, bordering on batshit crazy.

The pregnant woman, wearing a white coat, spoke to a man and pointed toward the waiting room. Eight other people sat in the space, most likely waiting on some kind of news about a loved one.

Nolan rested his head on the back of the chair. He'd told Jessica he'd meet her at his parents' house, though she was free to leave when his sister arrived since she'd Uber'd home over a half hour ago. Nearing the seventh month of her pregnancy, her exhaustion level was in high gear. His father still sat with his wife, and Nolan couldn't bring himself to force his father to leave.

They had the kind of love that great stories were written about.

He put the ring back in his pocket. He and Jessica had some time to figure things out. He certainly didn't want to scare her away.

"Mr. Nolan Greer?"

"Yes?" Nolan sat up, then stood as he faced a man who looked vaguely familiar. "Care to comment on the news about your girlfriend having been arrested for drug possession?"

"What?" Nolan rubbed his temples.

"Jessica Roads and the news she'd been arrested for possession?"

Nolan looked up at the man, still trying to decipher the meaning of the words and what it had to do with him, or Jessica. He looked vaguely familiar with his dark hair, notebook in hand... the press conference. The same reporter that asked him about his relationship with Jessica.

"What the fuck do you want?" Nolan barked.

"A statement about the latest report on Jessica Roads and her drug bust back in college."

The pounding between his ears echoed in

unison with his aching heart. "I have no idea what you are talking about, so I'd appreciate it if you—"

"It's all right here." The man held up his tablet. A mug shot of Jessica, obviously taken a few years back, graced the screen. The headline read:

JESSICA ROADS, *Social Media Director for the Miami Wildcats, has a Drug Record.*

"YOU FUCKING BASTARD!" Nolan cocked his arm, making a tight fist and landing it right on the reporter's nose. Blood squirted, hitting Nolan's shirt.

The reporter fell backward, landing on his ass.

Nolan leaned over. "Don't you have anything better to do besides digging up old dirt that doesn't mean jack shit?"

The pregnant woman raced to the reporter's side, helping him to a standing position. Had it not been for her, Nolan would have hit the asshole again.

Then it registered. "You!" He pointed to the pregnant woman. "You're married to Robert; the man Jessica was having an affair with. You're behind all this bullshit, aren't you?"

"I don't know what you are talking about." She took two steps backward.

Nolan waggled his finger. "I bet you're the person digging up all this crap, trying to make Jessica look bad because your husband cheated on you with her." He heard the words flying from his mouth, knowing he should shut the fuck up. "But I bet you had no idea that she didn't know he was married until it was too late. That he played her for a fool just like he did you." Painfully aware he stood next to a pregnant woman who dwarfed in his size, he stepped away from her but got closer to the prick asking the questions. "Tell me why you have it in for Jessica."

The reporter looked between him and the pregnant woman, that he knew for sure was Maggs, married to Robert. "Did she hire you to dig up gossip?"

A tall, slender man stomped down the hallway. "Back the hell away from my wife."

Robert. Fucking great.

"Back the fuck away from my girlfriend." Nolan took two strides before someone grabbed his biceps.

"Stop it right now," Jessica yelled.

"Your boyfriend is out of control," Robert said.

"Your hired asshat isn't very good." Jessica poked

Robert in the chest. "I saw him following me, and I also had my IT guys trace his IP address to a fake account that has been up my crotch all day."

Robert tossed his hands wide. "I have no idea what you're talking about."

"Maybe not. But your wife does, doesn't she?" Jessica said.

Nolan rubbed his face, retreating even farther away from the conflict. By the waiting room doors, he saw two men. One taking snapshots. The other with a video camera.

Fuck.

"You assholes deserve each other." Nolan waved his hand between the reporter and Robert and his wife. He glanced toward Jessica. "I don't have time right now for this shit." Without looking back, he took off down the hallway, looking for his father.

$\mathcal{I}$t had been three weeks since Nolan's mother had died and two weeks since he'd seen or talked to Jessica. He'd been appreciative of her presence and support during the days following his mother's death, especially where Heather had been concerned. Jessica had made a point to be with Heather whenever necessary, but Nolan noted how distant Jessica had become after the incident in the waiting room, which had been blown way out of proportion.

Actually, that was a false statement, though the truth had come out that Maggs had hired a crew of people to discredit Jessica in hopes to disgrace her and her career simply because she'd fallen for a lying cheat. The entire sordid affair had been put out there for public scrutiny. Mostly, it made Jessica look like a victim, but still, he understood her anger at the situation which is why he'd given her some space.

Then again, his family needed some time to grieve over the loss of his mother. Jessica had been by his side during the funeral, though they barely spoke. He'd taken a week off after the funeral only to come back to find out she'd taken two weeks off. Today when he'd called her, she texted back with: *Let's talk later in the week.*

He paced in her apartment building lobby for an hour waiting for her to come home. He knew she'd returned from visiting her parents because he'd seen her car in the parking lot at the stadium along with her gorgeous body in the stands during the opening game of the season, which ended five hours ago. Her reporting of the game and his coaching had been spot-on, but that wasn't why he wanted...no needed, to see her.

The ring burning a hole in his pocket and the love filling his heart demanded he speak with her. Now. Today. This second.

The last couple of weeks had been sheer hell.

The doors to the parking garage swung open, and Jessica stepped through. She stopped the moment her eyes connected with his. "Nolan," she said softly. Her sweet voice sent a warm tingle all over his skin.

God, how he missed her.

"What are you doing here?"

"We need to talk."

She nodded, stuffing a small bag into her purse. "I said later this week. We've both been busy."

"Heather wanted to sit with you at the game today. I thought you might have watched from the box. I was told that's where you usually did your reporting."

"I was in the box for part of the game and spoke with Heather for a bit. She's quite proud of her dad."

He hadn't known they'd seen each other since his father had taken his daughter home so Nolan could chase down the woman of his dreams and at the very least get rejected to his face. He swallowed. "Why are you ignoring me?" His heart pounded in his chest. His skin itched to scoop her into his arms and kiss her senseless.

"I told you after the funeral—"

"Yeah. I remember. Something about us both needing some time." He put his hands on his hips, sucking in a breath. His body trembled like the day he'd made the decision to retire. Fear prickled at the back of his neck. "Well, I'm tired of being ignored, so we're talking now."

"Fine," she said. "Let's go upstairs."

Once inside the elevator, he inched closer, pushing her against the wall. "Why have you been ignoring me?"

"I needed time to think. The scene at the hospital was intense and then the emotions around the funeral. We both needed time."

"I needed to step back from what happened in the hospital to help my father bury the love of his life. My family needed me, and I needed you. You did everything I asked, and I thought that meant you cared."

"I do, but—"

He hushed her with his forefinger. "After the funeral, I kept texting and calling, but you didn't answer. Heather and I needed you then too, but you took off. I gave you the space because I figured you needed it. What Robert and Maggs did, trying to destroy your reputation, sucked, and my punching the reporter that night certainly didn't help." He cupped her cheek, staring into her stunned eyes. "It's been hell without being able to do this." When he pressed his lips against hers, he moaned at the electric charge rippling between them.

Her hands came down hard on his chest, fists clenching his shirt. She pounded a second time as if to push him away, but her tongue swirled in his mouth in perfect harmony with his.

"I love you," he whispered in her ear. "I love you." He never wanted to stop saying those words to her, ever.

"What!?" She shoved him. "You did not just say you love me."

The elevator doors dinged open. He smiled, staring at her shocked face. "Come on. I think someone needs a glass of wine."

They stood in front of her apartment as she fumbled for her keys. Her hand shook as she opened the door. A pang of guilt for getting pleasure out of tossing her so off-kilter shot through his heart. But only a pang. A dollop of fear, however, raced through his veins.

He pushed back the door, and she tossed her purse toward the sofa, but missed, and the contents tumbled out to the floor.

"Shit," she muttered, lurching forward.

He grabbed her by her hips. "I've got it. You go pour yourself some wine, and then we can discuss the fact that we love each other."

"Oy," she whispered as she headed toward the kitchen.

He laughed as he collected her things, which included a small bag with a rectangular box. Just as he was about to stuff it in her bag, he saw these three letters through the clear plastic: EPT.

"You're pregnant?"

———————

"I DON'T KNOW," Jessica said as she poured Nolan a very large glass of wine. The moment her bag hit the floor and he insisted on picking the contents up, she knew this conversation was happening tonight whether she was pregnant or not. "But now you know part of why I was avoiding you. I wanted to wait until I knew for sure and had time to prepare whatever the fuck I was going to say if I am, and if I wasn't, then we could just talk about the fact we love each other."

"Oy," he repeated her word of a minute ago as he sat at the breakfast bar, taking the wine she offered and chugging half of it. "Guess I'm drinking alone tonight."

"Not necessarily. My period has never been regular. Just because I'm late doesn't mean I'm pregnant."

She watched him alternate between sipping his wine and scratching the back of his neck. "But the only way to find out for sure is to pee on the stick."

He let out a dry chuckle. "Come here."

Rotating the chair, he waggled his finger.

It was impossible not to smile when he had that devilish twinkle in his eye like a little boy about to play in the mud.

Why she'd been so afraid to be around him before taking the test, she had no idea. "I need you to know that my parents were really worried about me after the story broke. I had to go see them, and I had to focus on them. When I realized I was late, I panicked and didn't think I could be around you until I knew for sure."

He circled his arms around her waist, and it felt like she'd come home.

"I understand the first part of that statement, but you love me, which by the way, you have yet to say properly." He winked. "No matter what that test says, it won't change that I love you."

"I love you too," she whispered, smiling. "Crazy as it sounds."

"Not as crazy as what I'm about to do." His smile turned serious as he dug his hand into his pocket.

"This damn thing has been burning a hole in my pants since the night my mother died."

She cupped his face, kissing his lips. "I love you," she said again. "I like the way that rolls off my tongue."

"I like your tongue in my mouth." But instead of kissing her, he pushed back a tad.

She frowned.

He had the nerve to laugh. "Plenty of time for that later. Close your eyes."

She did as he asked.

"When I tell you to open them, I dare you to—"

"Don't dare me. The way I feel right now, I might have sex with you in public this time."

He laughed. "Open your eyes now and say yes."

Her stomach filled with butterflies as she blinked a few times. She expected to see him holding the pregnancy test and her saying yes meant she'd go take it. They needed to know one way or the other, and she also didn't know exactly how he felt about the prospects of her having his child. Of them having one together.

Hell, she didn't really know how she felt about the entire thing either.

She opened her mouth to say yes when her eyes

focused on a silver band holding one hell of a diamond.

"What the fuck?"

"That's not what I dared you to say."

She grabbed his shaking hand, holding it steady, getting a better look at the ring. "This isn't a joke."

He shook his head. "You're killing me. Say yes."

"You want to marry me?"

"That's half the reason I came over here tonight."

She kept looking between the ring pinched between his thumb and forefinger and his moist eyes. "Holy shit. I did not see this coming."

"Will you please put me out of my misery and say yes."

"Only I would get married on a dare." She nodded. "Yes."

He groaned as he pushed the ring on her finger. "It's my mother's ring."

Jessica gasped as she covered her mouth.

"She wanted you to have it, but I had to promise to treat you right."

"I'll hold you to that promise." She wrapped her arms around him, tucking her face in the crook of his neck. "Shall we find out if I'm going to be fat when I walk down the aisle?"

EPILOGUE

$\mathcal{N}$olan raced through the hospital, getting turned around twice as he tried to find the maternity ward. He nearly knocked over three people as he rounded the corner.

"Daddy!" Heather yelled from her wheelchair. Her surgery had been a success, and the recovery time would be close to a year, but the doctors were optimistic that this time she'd no longer need a brace.

"Where's Mommy?" He knelt in front of his daughter and ruffled her locks, giving her a kiss on the cheek. It had only been three months since Jessica had officially adopted Heather as her own. He thought it would take longer for Heather to call her mom, if ever, but she started before the adoption came through.

"She's in a birthing room," his father said. "Down the hall, second door. Karen is with her, but I'll warn you, your wife—"

"Mommy's swearing a lot." Heather scrunched up her nose.

"Something about back labor," his father said.

He had no idea what that was and wasn't sure he wanted to find out. "Guess I better go find my wife."

He found the room, though as he walked down the hallway, he heard all sorts of moaning and yelling, and none of it sounded pleasant.

"Jessica?" He pushed back the door to see his wife on all fours, his sister rubbing something across her back. A nurse looked at some paper coming out of a machine. He had half a mind to turn around and walk right out that door.

"This position is how we got ourselves in this fucking mess to begin with," Jessica said...more like panted as she did the breathing they'd learned in the birthing classes.

"That's my cue to leave." His sister waved him over, showing him how to roll the object along Jessica's back. "It's been difficult from the moment her water broke, but the good news is she's dilating quickly, so it shouldn't be too long," Karen whispered before leaving the room.

Jessica groaned, pounding the hospital bed with her fist.

"Breathe, babe," Nolan said, conjuring up everything he could remember from the classes. He leaned closer to her face, making eye contact and breathing with her.

"She isn't getting any break between contractions," the nurse said, pointing to her paper. "This here shows the peak, then you can see it never subsides. The doctor should be in any minute to check on things."

Nolan focused on rubbing Jessica's back, breathing with her, and not taking anything that came out of her mouth personally.

About ten minutes later, the doctor arrived. Nolan helped Jessica to her back. Tears burned the corners of his eyes. One broken condom and the woman he loved was in excruciating pain. He knew the end result would be another baby, but still, it broke his heart to see her like this. He took a cool cloth and brushed the perspiration away from her face, which at that moment was turning beet red.

"Doc, I think something is wrong." Panic

squeezed his heart as Jessica stared at him with wide eyes.

"Nothing's wrong," the doctor said calmly. "Jessica, keep pushing, the baby's head is crowning."

"What!?"

Jessica took in a deep breath, then held it, pulling her legs up.

Nolan honestly, for the first time in his life, had no idea what to do.

"That's it, Jessica. One big long push," the doctor said. "Dad, if you want to see your baby born, I suggest you look down here."

Nolan kissed Jessica's forehead, holding her hand, and chose to watch from her angle.

"Oh...my...God," he whispered as the doctor rotated the baby's head, shifting one shoulder out and then the other. His baby's arms and legs twitched as it let out a bloodcurdling wail.

"It's a boy," Jessica whispered as she raised her arms, waggling her fingers.

Nolan stepped back in awe as the doctor placed his baby on Jessica's chest.

The next twenty minutes went by in a haze. Nolan cut the cord. A team of doctors and nurses checked the baby over and attended to his wife while he sat in a chair next to Jessica, holding her hand, kissing her lips, and crying. Not sobbing, but tears burned down his cheeks.

One of the nurses handed Jessica their son, swaddled tight in a blanket with a little white cap over his head. "Nine pounds, eight ounces and twenty-three inches long."

"That's a big boy," Nolan said with pride.

"Thanks for the reminder, honey."

Nolan winced.

Jessica laughed. "As if you had any clue what that felt like."

"I imagine I never really want to know." He kissed his son's pudgy cheek. "We need a name for this little guy."

"Heather and I came up with Hunter Nolan Greer."

"I like It." Nolan pressed his lips against hers. Their tongues tangled together with the promise of the kind of love that lasts forever. "I love you," Nolan whispered. "Thanks for daring to kiss me."

Thank you for reading TAKING A RISK. Please feel free to leave an honest review.

I'm super excited to announce I'm writing a new series with NY Times Bestselling Author Elle James.

First book will be released May 6, 2025. Check it out.

Secrets in Calusa Cove

GRAB A GLASS OF VINO, kick back, relax, and let the romance roll in...

Sign up for my *Newsletter (https://dl.bookfunnel. com/82gm8b9k4y) where I often give away free books before publication.*

JOIN *my private Facebook group (https://www.facebook. com/groups/191706547909047/) where I post exclusive excerpts and discuss all things murder and love!*

ABOUT THE AUTHOR

Jen Talty is the *USA Today* Bestselling Author of Contemporary Romance, Romantic Suspense, and Paranormal Romance. In the fall of 2020, her short story was selected and featured in a 1001 Dark Nights Anthology.

Regardless of the genre, her goal is to take you on a ride that will leave you floating under the sun with warmth in your heart. She writes stories about broken heroes and heroines who aren't necessarily looking for romance, but in the end, they find the kind of love books are written about :).

She first started writing while carting her kids to one hockey rink after the other, averaging 170 games per year between 3 kids in 2 countries and 5 states. Her first book, IN TWO WEEKS was originally published in 2007. In 2010 she helped form a publishing company (Cool Gus Publishing) with *NY*

Times Bestselling Author Bob Mayer where she ran the technical side of the business through 2016.

Jen is currently enjoying the next phase of her life... the empty nester! She and her husband reside in Jupiter, Florida.

Grab a glass of vino, kick back, relax, and let the romance roll in...

Sign up for my Newsletter (https://dl.bookfunnel. com/82gm8b9k4y) where I often give away free books before publication.

Join my private Facebook group (https://www.facebook. com/groups/191706547909047/) where I post exclusive excerpts and discuss all things murder and love!

Never miss a new release. Follow me on Amazon: amazon.com/author/jentalty

And on Bookbub: bookbub.com/authors/jen-talty

ALSO BY JEN TALTY

Brand New Series Co-Written With Elle James!

Welcome to...Everglades Overwatch!

Secrets in Calusa Cove

Safe Harbor Series

Mine To Keep

Mine To Save

Mine To Protect

Mine to Hold

Mine to Love

Check out LOVE IN THE ADIRONDACKS!

Shattered Dreams

An Inconvenient Flame

The Wedding Driver

Clear Blue Sky

Blue Moon

Before the Storm

NY STATE TROOPER SERIES (also set in the Adirondacks!)

In Two Weeks

Dark Water

Deadly Secrets

Murder in Paradise Bay

To Protect His own

Deadly Seduction

When A Stranger Calls

His Deadly Past

The Corkscrew Killer

First Responders: A spin-off from the NY State Troopers series

Playing With Fire

Private Conversation

The Right Groom

After The Fire

Caught In The Flames

Chasing The Fire

Legacy Series

Dark Legacy

Legacy of Lies

Secret Legacy

Emerald City

Investigate Away

Sail Away

Fly Away

Flirt Away

Hawaii Brotherhood Protectors

Waylen Unleashed

Bowie's Battle

Colorado Brotherhood Protectors

Fighting For Esme

Defending Raven

Fay's Six

Darius' Promise

Yellowstone Brotherhood Protectors

Guarding Payton

Wyatt's Mission

Corbin's Mission

Candlewood Falls

Rivers Edge

The Buried Secret

Its In His Kiss

Lips Of An Angel

Kisses Sweeter than Wine

A Little Bit Whiskey

It's all in the Whiskey

Johnnie Walker

Georgia Moon

Jack Daniels

Jim Beam

Whiskey Sour

Whiskey Cobbler

Whiskey Smash

Irish Whiskey

The Monroes

Color Me Yours

Color Me Smart

Color Me Free

Color Me Lucky

Color Me Ice

Color Me Home

Search and Rescue

Protecting Ainsley

Protecting Clover

Protecting Olympia

Protecting Freedom

Protecting Princess

Protecting Marlowe

Fallport Rescue Operations

Searching for Madison

Searching for Haven

Searching for Pandora

Searching for Stormi

DELTA FORCE-NEXT GENERATION

Shielding Jolene

Shielding Aalyiah

Shielding Laine

Shielding Talullah

Shielding Maribel

Shielding Daisy

The Men of Thief Lake

Rekindled

Destiny's Dream

Federal Investigators

Jane Doe's Return

The Butterfly Murders

THE AEGIS NETWORK

The Sarich Brother

The Lighthouse

Her Last Hope

The Last Flight

The Return Home

The Matriarch

Aegis Network: Jacksonville Division

A SEAL's Honor

Talon's Honor

Arthur's Honor

Rex's Honor

Kent's Honor

Buddy's Honor

Aegis Network Short Stories

Max & Milian

A Christmas Miracle

Spinning Wheels

Holiday's Vacation

The Brotherhood Protectors

Out of the Wild

Rough Justice

Rough Around The Edges

Rough Ride

Rough Edge

Rough Beauty

The Brotherhood Protectors

The Saving Series

Saving Love

Saving Magnolia

Saving Leather

Hot Hunks

Cove's Blind Date Blows Up

My Everyday Hero – Ledger

Tempting Tavor

Malachi's Mystic Assignment

Needing Neor

Holiday Romances

A Christmas Getaway

Alaskan Christmas

Whispers

Christmas In The Sand

Heroes & Heroines on the Field

Taking A Risk

Tee Time

A New Dawn

The Blind Date

Spring Fling

Summers Gone

Winter Wedding

The Awakening

Fated Moons

The Collective Order

The Lost Sister

The Lost Soldier

The Lost Soul

The Lost Connection

The New Order

www.ingramcontent.com/pod-product-compliance
Lightning Source LLC
Chambersburg PA
CBHW010738130726
47899CB00015B/3413